ADELINA

Twenty years after the events described in Sarah, the daughter of Lady Caroline and Thomas Cole returns to Abbeyford. The first person she meets is Lord Lynwood who once loved her mother... Twenty years on, Evan Smithson, the illegitimate son of Sarah and Guy Trent, wants revenge against all the Trents. His actions touch not only his half brother Wallis Trent, but the lives of Adelina and Lord Lynwood.

ADELINA

ADELINA

by

Margaret Dickinson

Magna Large Print Books
Long Preston, North Yorkshire,
England.

British Library Cataloguing in Publication Data.

Dickinson, Margaret
Adelina.

A catalogue record for this book is available from the British Library

ISBN 0-7505-0788-8

First published in Great Britain by Robert Hale Ltd., 1981

Published in Large Print June, 1996 by arrangement with Darley Anderson.

Magna Large Print is an imprint of
Library Magna Books Ltd.
Printed and bound in Great Britain by
T.J. Press (Padstow) Ltd., Cornwall, PL28 8RW.

The Abbeyford Trilogy

Sarah—

How it all began! How Sarah—a village milkmaid—becomes personal maid to Lady Caroline. Sarah's love affair with the squire's son, Guy Trent, can only end in tragedy that will reach across three generations. Equally foolish is Lady Caroline's passion for the estate bailiff, Thomas Cole—but she is more determined, more ruthless and means to have her own way...

Adelina—

Twenty years later, the daughter of Lady Caroline and Thomas Cole returns to Abbeyford and the first person she meets is Lord Lynwood. Lynwood—who had once loved her mother...

Twenty years on—Evan Smithson, the illegitimate son of Sarah and Guy Trent, and his lust for revenge against all the Trents, touches not only his half-brother, Wallis Trent, but casts a shadow over the lives of Adelina and Lord Lynwood.

Carrie—

'Why have we come to Abbeyford?' Carrie asks her father, Evan Smithson. 'I've unfinished business hereabouts!' Evan's revenge against the Trents is not yet complete. Sarah's granddaughter, Carrie, and Guy's grandson, Jamie Trent, fall desperately in love—but Evan stands between them. Carrie marries Lloyd Foster, though after his death she again searches for Jamie. She follows him to the Crimea, but, believing him to be dead, she returns to Abbeyford where she had once found the only true happiness she had ever known.

Abbeyford where it had all begun so long ago...

CHAPTER 1

New York Harbour, 1815

Adelina Cole rubbed away the grime on the window with her fingers and peered into the tavern. She could see her father sitting in the far corner with three of his so-called friends, drinking and gambling as usual.

She sighed and shivered as a gust of wind blew along the wooden verandah. Pulling the torn shawl closer around her shoulders, Adelina glanced fearfully towards the harbour. She could see the forest of ships' masts lining the piers, swaying more than normal. The black sky overhead warned of a gathering storm. Adelina bit her lip. She did not know which frightened her the most—the threatening thunderstorm or the inmates of the waterfront tavern!

But, to get to the room where she and her father lived above the bar, she would have to go in. If only Sam, the owner, did not see her and insist that she serve his customers as payment of rent arrears.

She leaned her head against the rough wood and closed her eyes, momentarily overcome by the weariness of the daily struggle—hour by hour—to survive.

She opened her eyes again and they focused upon her father. Even from this distance she could see the hand in which he held his cards shaking. His eyes were bloodshot and bleary, blinking rapidly, and he stretched his face from time to time as if he could not see clearly. Nor could he, she thought, not without a little impatience, for one eye was half-closed and surrounded by purple bruising from last night's fight.

Every night it was the same. The drink, the gambling—and then the quarrels. Drunken, ugly brawls and always Thomas Cole, weak and sick and vulnerable, came out of them bruised and beaten. Adelina was frightened. Not for herself, but for him. Frightened that one night, one drink too many or one punch too hard, would really harm him.

Life was hard on the New York waterfront and lives were cheap. There'd be no one to care—except his daughter.

Adelina fingered the silver locket about her neck. It was the only thing left in their harsh life that reminded her of earlier, happier days. She had worn the locket for the past four months, ever since she had found it.

One night while helping her father on to the shake-down on the floor of their room, as she had removed his jacket—struggling with his helpless, sprawling limbs—she had felt something hard sewn into the lining of his coat. When she had examined it closely, she found the stitching, though ill-formed and untidy, was tight and strong as if concealing more worth than the whole threadbare coat itself. As she had fingered the small, hard object, her eyes had lingered upon the prostrate form of her father, his head lolling to one side, his mouth wide open, snoring in uneven, rasping bursts. Adelina had sighed and shaken her head sadly. What an ugly sight he had become, and yet he was so pathetic.

It had taken her three days to prise the truth from her father, to persuade him to cut open the stitching and show her the object. His shaking fingers dropped the heart-shaped locket into her hands. 'It was your mother's, she always wore it.' He sniffed. 'It's the only thing I have left of hers.' He paused, then said reluctantly, 'I suppose you'd better have it.'

Adelina thought cynically that it would be safer in her possession, so she did not persuade him to keep it. Silently she fastened the tarnished chain about her neck. Then she opened the locket and twisted it to look at the tiny pictures within.

'Who are they? Not—not you and Mama?'

'No—her people. Her parents.' He jabbed a grubby finger at the locket. 'My Lord and Lady Royston, they are.'

'Who?' Adelina's green eyes widened.

'Robert Elcombe, the Earl of Royston, of Abbeyford—a little village near Manchester in the Old Country.' Thomas Cole's bleary eyes watered at the memory of far-off days. 'He's her father. Her mother's dead—died before I even knew her.'

'And—and her father?'

He shrugged and then flopped back on the shake-down and closed his eyes. 'How the hell should I know!' he muttered.

Within seconds he was snoring loudly, whilst Adelina still gazed at the faces in the locket.

Now as she stood peering in through

the dirty window, fingering the locket, her thoughts were interrupted as the swing doors flew open and a man came hurtling through the air to land in a sprawling heap almost at her feet. Another figure sprang through the doors and leapt on top of the man on the ground and began smashing his fists into his face. Such drunken fights were commonplace and Adelina was untroubled by it. She saw the disturbance only as a means by which she might succeed in slipping through the saloon and up the stairs unobserved.

She was about halfway to the stairs when she felt someone grip her arm and, turning, found young Sammy's blue eyes gazing up at her.

If there was anyone in this awful place who was a friend to her then it was the tavern owner's young, ill-treated son, Sammy. The fourteen-year-old boy looked only eleven, his tattered clothes hanging loosely on his thin body. He worked hard but received nothing for his efforts but abuse and his father's fist. Right now his eye was beginning to colour from yet another vicious cuff.

'What is it, Sammy?' Adelina asked him gently.

'Your Pa's sure gettin' himself in deep trouble, Miss Adelina. He ain't no match for those card-sharps.'

Adelina sighed and glanced through the haze of smoke towards her father. She hesitated between reaching the safety of their one room and rescuing her befuddled father from the men who would cheat him out of the ragged shirt on his back.

She hesitated a moment too long.

'Aha, Miss Adelina.' Big Sam was approaching. A fat, cruel-looking man, his only aim in life was to make money with no scruples as to how he made it. His right arm swept in an arc and knocked young Sammy off his feet, but he did not even glance down at his son.

'Leave the boy alone,' Adelina faced the big man angrily, but he only laughed.

'Ah, you're sure lovely when you're angry.' His grip fastened upon her arm and he pushed his ugly face close to hers. 'You'll serve my customers their drinks, miss, and make like you kinda want to, or,' he jerked his thumb towards her father in the corner, 'I'll see him in the jail.'

Big Sam's threat was no idle one, for he'd put her father in jail twice before for debt and kept her working for him to pay off twice the amount which was owed.

As always, his threat brought her rebellion under control, but strengthened her iron resolve to escape from this man's clutches, even if she had to drag her father bodily with her. She would not—could not—desert Thomas Cole, for in her heart there were still the memories of better times.

The memory of her mother's lovely face and her father's smile; of a warm bed; of food and new clothes; of soft hands and a gentle voice; of happiness. For the most part the memories were faint, elusive, obliterated by the harsh reality of the present, yet at times they came flooding back into her mind strong and clear to revive her spirit and help her to fight all the harder for their existence. She had to struggle for the both of them, for Thomas Cole had lost the will to live with the death of his beloved Caroline some nine years earlier. Only Adelina's will-power kept him alive. From a genteel, sheltered little girl, she had, of necessity, had to become a fighter, a survivor and protector of her father. From her parents, Adelina had inherited their best qualities—strength without selfishness, gentleness and compassion without weakness.

There was a commotion in her father's corner. The table overturned and drinks were spilled.

'You're a liar and a cheat, Thomas Cole!'

Her father sat in his chair, slumped forward. Four days' growth of beard upon his chin, his hair long and dirty, his eyes bloodshot. Adelina's heart turned over at the sight of him. Objectively, she couldn't understand why she stood by him, supported him, worked for him. Yet he was her father. He was all she had right now. She moved towards him, but the man who had yelled abuse at him now caught hold of the neck of his shirt and hoisted Thomas to his feet. For a few seconds he held him aloft. Thomas, stupefied, hung there limply, his head lolling to one side, his eyes rolling. The man brought his right arm back and clenched his fist.

As Adelina cried out, 'No, oh no!' his fist smashed into her father's face, snapping his head back with a sickening crack. The man loosened his hold on him and Thomas Cole fell backwards hitting his head on the table with a dull thud.

Several other men now rose to their feet, their shouts only adding to the confusion. Adelina tried to push her way through them to reach her father, but they pressed round the scene, blocking her path.

Suddenly, their raucous shouts died away and there was an uncanny silence.

'*Jesus!*' someone said, 'you've killed him.'

Frantic now, Adelina fought her way through. The man was standing over her father, who was lying in a twisted heap at his feet. Blood trickled from Thomas Cole's mouth and from a gash on his temple. Adelina threw herself upon her knees beside him. She took hold of his hand and chafed it. Her eyes flashed angrily towards her father's assailant.

'You're a brute, Jed Hawkins. You'll swing for that fist of yours yet.'

'Seems like he will now,' muttered someone. 'Yer sure seen him off.'

Jed stood there looking stupid. 'I didn't mean to kill him, Miss Adelina. It's just that the silly old fool was playing his cards all wrong. I guess he was too drunk to see them...'

'Oh, shut up and help me carry him upstairs. I must bathe his head and...'

'Tain't no use, Miss Adelina.' Another of the men put his hand upon her shoulder with a rough tenderness. 'Don't you understand what we're sayin'? He's a gone. He's dead!'

For a moment Adelina stared at the man.

'No—oh, no,' she whispered and then slowly turned to look down at the still form. She was rigidly motionless for some moments, while the men watched with uneasy silence.

Trembling a little, she reached out her hand and slid it beneath his shirt. There was no heartbeat.

As they had said, her father was dead.

Adelina bowed her head on to his lifeless chest and wept. Tears of bitterness, tears of remorse, tears of grief.

She became aware of feet shuffling near her and of the mutterings.

'That sure weren't no fair fight, no sir!'

'You oughta be hanged, Jed.'

'Hittin' the poor ole begger and him drunk and senseless.'

'What about the girl?'

'Guess Sam'll take care o' her.' There were a few half-hearted guffaws.

Death came quickly and often in this

neighbourhood and was swiftly forgotten by those not directly involved.

Sam! The name penetrated her distraught mind and Adelina scrambled to her feet. There was nothing more she could do for her father.

Now she must save herself...

Too late, for Sam himself was shouldering his way through the throng. Wildly, she looked about her for a way of escape but there was none. He stood, legs apart, over the corpse and laughed, his great, fat belly shaking with mirth.

The tears dried in Adelina's eyes as grief gave way to rage. With a shriek she hurled herself at Sam and pummelled her fists against his chest, but he gripped her wrists and held her easily. So she kicked his legs and bit his hand. She screamed and kicked and scratched, venting her anger and grief upon this hateful man who had been the supplier of the drink which had ruined her father and had held her captive by the subsequent debt.

How she hated and feared this brute who could not even treat his own son properly.

'You've a handful there, Sam,' someone shouted.

Sam laughed. 'I'll tame the she-cat. She'll come a-crawlin' soon enough.' He dealt her a vicious blow with the back of his hand. 'I'll lock you in your room, miss, until you've come to your senses.'

Huddled on the shake-down, the bruise on her temple swelling rapidly, Adelina fingered the locket about her neck.

England, she thought, if I can get away from Sam, I'll go to England and seek out Mama's home.

There was a scrabbling at the door and the rusty key turned in the lock and young Sammy's spikey hair appeared round the door. 'Quick, Miss Adelina, he's out the back. You can get out while he's gone.'

Adelina scrambled to her feet, snatched her shawl and the bundle of her few items of clothing from the corner and followed Sammy down the stairs, through the now empty saloon bar and out into the wild night.

He took her hand and dragged her along the street. The wind whistled, plucking at her skirt, threatening to tear away her shawl, but bending her head against the storm she followed Sammy.

Breathlessly, they fell into a sheltered

corner near the harbour. The storm was overhead and Adelina's teeth began to chatter with fear. She hated storms.

Sammy cupped his hands around his mouth and spoke close to her ear. 'If you can get on a ship, you could get right away from here. It'd be the best way. By road, he'd catch up with you.'

Adelina nodded. 'I could go to England, but I've no money.'

Sammy shrugged. 'No problem. Stow away.' He suggested in a matter-of-fact manner.

'But—but how do I know which ship is going to England?' Adelina's eyes flickered down the long line of swaying masts.

Sammy said, 'Look you stay here, I'll go along the harbour an' see if I can find out if there's one bound for England.'

He was gone a long time, so long that Adelina began to think he had deserted her and returned home. She crouched behind a stack of barrels, trying to find a little shelter. Then the rain came, soaking in minutes her thin shawl. She shivered from cold and fear, and delayed shock. She groaned aloud, the picture of her father's still form horribly fresh in her mind.

Sammy was back, squeezing his thin

frame between the barrels. 'Miss Adelina, where are you? Oh, there you are. I've found one,' he told her gleefully. 'Come on, I'll take you. It sails on the tide. If we go now, there's no one about, the crew are all having a last fling ashore. If you slip on now and hide yourself in one of those longboats they have on deck, no one'll find you.'

'But—but I can't stay hidden under there all the way to England. It takes weeks!'

'I've thought about that,' answered the practical Sammy and gestured towards a bundle in his hand. 'I've gotten you some food. Stay hidden as long as you can, then if they find you when they're at sea it'll be too late anyway,' he said triumphantly. 'They'll not turn back just to put you ashore.'

'I suppose not,' Adelina said doubtfully, 'but—but what do they do to stowaways? Flog them?'

'Naw,' scoffed Sammy, 'not a pretty girl, anyway. Likely as not they'll make a fuss of you,' he added with a confidence Adelina did not share. The young boy, old for his years though his hard life had made him in many ways, could not be expected to understand the fears of a young girl amongst a group of rough, tough sailors.

Adelina swallowed her fear. The prospects of a life under big Sam's rule were even worse. She would take the risk. She would do anything, risk anything, to get away from Big Sam.

'What about you, Sammy, aren't you going to come with me?'

'No, Miss Adelina. I'll get away from him one day, but I want to head west. I gotten it all figured out. When I'm a bit older...' He grinned at her, for a moment no longer the half-starved waif, but a boy with determination and toughness. Adelina felt relief. Sammy would be all right.

Adelina remained hidden for the first four days of the voyage. Luckily she did not suffer sea-sickness and, though the small, stuffy space beneath a tarpaulin covering a longboat was cramped and unpleasant, there she stayed.

On the fourth day, when the sun was high in the sky, two sailors pulled back the tarpaulin.

Adelina blinked in the sudden bright light.

'Gawd love us! Look what we 'ave 'ere!' cried one.

The other one gaped. 'A stowaway!' Then he grinned with blackened teeth. 'An' a mighty pretty one too, ain't she?'

'I saw 'er first, Black Wilf,' said the first.

'Mebbe, but you owes me for savin' yer miserable life in that fight we 'ad in New York harbour, don't forgit.'

Suddenly a knife blade flashed in the sunlight and Adelina watched with horrified eyes as the two ruffians faced each other, circling like two wary fighting cocks.

'She's mine, I tell 'ee.'

'You owes me.'

'What's this?' roared a deep voice. It was the First Mate bearing down upon the sailors. 'No fightin' aboard this ship.' He stopped in astonishment as he caught sight of Adelina.

'Good grief!' He stared at her open-mouthed.

'She'm a stowaway, Mister Mate.'

'An' I saw 'er first. She's mine. Warm my hammock a treat.'

As Black Wilf growled again, the First Mate said, 'She'll warm no one's hammock. She'll be dealt with by the Cap'n.'

'Aw, come on, Mister Mate...'

'Silence!' The Mate roared and even Adelina jumped and began to feel more afraid than she had at the mercy of the two seamen.

'Come on, out with you,' the Mate flicked his hand towards her.

Stiffly, her limbs cramped and cold, she climbed out of her hiding-place. Not one of the watching men stepped forward to offer her his helping hand.

'Come with me.' The Mate turned abruptly and Adelina followed him meekly. The sailors, now united in their disappointment in losing her to their superior, shouted after her.

'Lucky Cap'n with you in his bed the night!'

Adelina bit her lip, regretting her hasty, thoughtless flight from New York just to escape from Big Sam. Doubtless the world was littered with the likes of Big Sam! Perhaps the Captain...

Below, the Mate knocked upon a cabin door and pushed her in front of him.

'Cap'n. We have a stowaway.' The man who looked up from the chart he was studying spread out on the table in the centre of the small cabin, was tall, broad, but with a tell-tale middle-aged paunch.

His face was half-covered by a beard and moustache, but his eyes were sharp and bright in the weatherbeaten, leathery face.

He grunted and straightened, his cool eyes looking Adelina up and down. 'Well, missy, and where did you think you were going?'

With a brave defiance she did not feel inwardly, Adelina held her head high. 'England! My grandfather is the Earl of Royston.'

A huge bellow of laughter welled up inside the man and he threw back his head and roared. 'Hear that, Mister Mate? We have a *lady* aboard!'

'Aye, Cap'n,' the Mate grinned.

Adelina glared resentfully at the Captain.

'Well, missy, I admire your courage. 'Tis a pity you're not a man. You'd make a fine seaman, eh, Mister Mate?'

'Aye, Cap'n.'

'Well, now,' the Captain said, controlling his mirth at last. 'What to do with you?' He pondered for a moment, looking at her reflectively. 'Can you cook, girl?'

'Yes—yes I can.'

'Good. Our ship's cook's gone down with the fever this very day. You,' he prodded his finger at her, 'can take his place.'

So Adelina passed the voyage as ship's cook! She had been very fortunate to find a Captain, not only with a sense of humour who treated her presence aboard his ship as a huge joke, but one who was also a god-fearing gentleman who minded that she was kept safe from his lusty crew!

CHAPTER 2

' 'Ere you be, miss.' The tinker pulled his laden cart to a jingling, tinkling halt. 'This 'ere's Amberly. I stops 'ere. O'er yonder, see that wood?'

Adelina shaded her eyes against the summer sun. 'Yes—yes, I see it.'

'Go through that there wood, and down t'hill and you'm in Abbeyford. Lord Royston lives at Abbeyford Grange on t'opposite side. Big place, you'm can't miss it.'

'Thank you for the ride,' she said, climbing down from the cart and giving his mangy old mule an affectionate pat.

The flies buzzed around the animal's head so that his ears were constantly twitching and his tail swishing, but in vain in the August heat. 'Poor old thing, you're sure hot, aren't you?' She sighed. 'So am I.' She looked down at her old skirt, dusty and badly stained. 'I can hardly meet my grandfather like this,' she murmured, 'but I guess there's not much I can do about it.'

Although she had been confiding her thoughts to the mule, the tinker's sharp ears missed nothing.

' 'Ere, ain't you no other dress but that 'un?'

Adelina grinned up at him. 'I'm afraid not. He'll just have to take me as I am.'

The tinker sniffed and rummaged in a box behind him. He pulled out a pale blue silk dress, high-waisted with puffed sleeves and a low neckline. 'Will this fit you?' He pushed it at her.

She held it up before her, her eyes sparkling. It was crumpled and had a small tear at the hem, but it was a vast improvement on the garments she wore. 'Yes—but I've no money.' She held it out to him. 'I'm sorry—I can't pay you.'

'G'arn,' he sniffed. 'You'm been company

on the road here from Liverpool. Tek it.'

'Are you sure?' Adelina said doubtfully, but still holding the garment, secretly longing to keep it, but the tinker looked scarcely any wealthier than herself!

He grinned toothlessly at her. 'Well, I ain't no use for it, an' folks round here won't buy it, it's a sight too fancy for country women.'

'Well—if you're sure—thank's a lot.'

The dry dust rose in little puffs as she walked along the meandering lane and Adelina was thankful to reach the shade of the wood. She was so hot and sticky and thirsty. She dropped down into the grass, leant against a tree and closed her eyes, but her mouth and throat were so dry. In the quiet of the wood she listened intently.

Amidst the birdsong and the rustling of scurrying little creatures through the undergrowth, Adelina could hear the sound of water. She licked her dry lips and swallowed, her throat sore. The sound seemed to come from her left so she rose and followed the narrow, winding path through the trees until the way fell steeply downwards. The noise of the waterfall was louder now. Eagerly, Adelina slipped and slithered down the path and gasped with sheer delight as she came upon the waterfall and the rocky pool.

Scrambling feverishly over the rocks, she cupped her hands beneath the sparkling water and drank and drank. Then she splashed it over her hot face. Thirst satisfied, she sat down upon a rock and watched the waterfall in fascination. It was cooler here, beside the water and beneath the shade of the overhanging trees, but she still felt hot and dirty. She spread out the dress the tinker had given her on a rock and eyed the deep, inviting pool longingly. Without really making a conscious decision, she peeled off her clothing and jumped into the water. She gave a little squeal of surprise and pleasure, the water was colder than she had expected, but lovely, deliciously cooling! She splashed and dived and shook her head like a playful puppy, enjoying the freedom, the freshness.

Riding through the wood on his way home, Francis Amberly, seventh Earl of Lynwood since the death of his father twenty-three years earlier, heard faintly Adelina's squeals of delight. Quietly, he swung down from his horse and leaving the trustworthy animal, he ran softly between the trees until he came out at the edge of the rock face overlooking the pool. For some moments, he watched the lovely naked water nymph splashing in the water. In a patch of sunlight filtering through the trees, she raised her wet face to the warmth, hair plastered darkly to her head, eyes closed, lips parted in sheer ecstasy.

Lynwood felt a strange constriction in his chest, the scene reeling before his eyes. He grasped hold of the branch of a tree to steady himself.

No! No—it wasn't possible!

He passed his hand across his eyes as if in disbelief. But when he looked again, she was still there. This girl—was real!

Caroline had come back!

No—no, he told himself firmly, half angry with himself for such whimsical thoughts. That was twenty years ago. This was a young girl—but so like Caroline it was hardly credible.

He watched as she climbed from the pool, her lovely body glistening, her long hair wet and shining. He watched as she dried herself with her shawl, and dressed. He saw her stand, half clothed in her chemise, holding the blue dress up, inspecting it critically. To Lynwood's eyes it was a poor rag of a gown, but the girl seemed pleased by what she saw, and a small smile curved his lips as she slipped the garment over her head and wriggled into it. Still he watched as she found a rock to sit on where the sun shone warmly through the trees, and began to rub her hair dry. Unable to move, he gazed in fascination, knowing even before it happened, that as the seemingly black, wet hair dried, it would become the lovely auburn colour of Caroline's hair!

The nymph stood up and, as if feeling his eyes upon her, she turned and slowly surveyed the edge of the rock face above her.

As soon as she saw him, her lips parted in a gasp and the colour slowly crept up her neck and suffused her face. Then embarrassment was replaced by indignation. Hands on hips, she demanded, 'How long have you been standing there?'

Her voice was not Caroline's, though everything else about her, from her auburn hair, her green eyes, now sparkling angrily, to her lovely, curving body was Caroline. It was incredible! Not possible!

But the voice was different. Caroline's

had been high-pitched, rather affected. This girl's was low and husky and her speech held the faint drawl of the Americas.

'Quite some time,' he said.

They stared at each other. Adelina—in spite of her discomfort—noticed that he was a handsome man, obviously a gentleman with a broad brow and a long, aquiline nose. He wore a short riding-jacket, with a high-collared shirt and a casually tied neckcloth, close-fitting breeches and black, knee-high riding-boots. His tall hat was set at a jaunty angle and as he stood looking down at her, a sardonic smile curving his lips, he idly slapped his riding-crop against his boot.

'Well, if you've quite finished?' she said drily, smoothing down the skirt of her recent acquisition, and picking up the bundle of her old clothes. 'I'll be on my way.'

She climbed up the path and as she made to pass, close by, he reached out and his fingers closed about her arm.

Her green eyes flashed contempt into his blue, mocking gaze.

'Don't run away, my lovely water-nymph,' he smiled.

'How *dare* you?' she cried, knowing

now that he had most certainly observed her bathing. Against her will, her blush deepened.

'Where are you going, anyway?'

She flung back her head and retorted, 'To Abbeyford to meet my grandfather—the Earl of Royston,' she added grandly, hoping to impress him.

His grasp upon her arm, tightened, his fingers digging into her flesh. He pulled her closer to him. Looking down into Caroline's eyes, Caroline's face—and yet it was not Caroline—he demanded harshly, 'Who *are* you?'

'Adelina—Adelina Cole.'

Although he was half expecting such an answer, the shock still showed in his face.

'Her daughter!' he muttered.

'I beg your pardon?'

'Nothing!' he snapped and released his hold on her abruptly. He seemed about to turn away from her, but hesitated saying, 'You'll find no welcome at Abbeyford Grange.'

Adelina waited, the questions tumbling about her mind, but something about this man's attitude silenced her—almost frightened her. He seemed to be battling with some inner conflict.

She watched him, her head on one side then said quietly, 'You know him?'

'Yes. Yes, I do. And he'll not want to see you. You're too like your—mother!'

Adelina's eyes shone and she asked eagerly, 'My mother? You knew my mother?'

Lynwood glanced at her and then looked quickly away. 'Oh, yes—I knew her.' There was bitterness in his voice.

The sight of Adelina—so like Caroline—had brought back a tumult of emotions Lord Lynwood had thought buried along with his boyhood. It was as if a ghost stood before him, the object of his boyhood affections, the subject of his adolescent dreams—the one who had, by her cruel deceit, destroyed his adoration, and his belief in women. And yet he could not turn away from this girl, so obviously alone and impoverished. She was Caroline's daughter—he should turn and flee! Grudgingly, half knowing as he did so that he was lost, he said, 'Look—I'd better take you home with me, to Lynwood Hall, for the time being. Perhaps my mother will know what's best to do with you.'

'Lordy me, Francis, what on earth have

you picked up here? A scarecrow?' Then Lady Lynwood peered more closely at the girl her son had brought into her luxurious sitting-room. The same surprise Adelina had seen in Lynwood's eyes was mirrored in his mother's but this time there was no pain accompanying it. 'I don't need to ask who *you* are!'

The old lady's eyes appraised her from head to foot. Adelina held her head defiantly high and met Lady Lynwood's gaze boldly. She seemed, to Adelina, to be incredibly old—a tiny figure dressed entirely in black with a wide, voluminous skirt, a jet necklace and ear-rings. Her hair was completely white and her olive skin very wrinkled, but her eyes were bright and alert and now twinkled with sudden mischief as she looked at her son. 'I dare say she'd be quite presentable properly dressed. Has he seen her?'

Lynwood shook his head.

'My word—he's in for a shock! What's your name?'

'Adelina Cole.'

The old lady nodded slowly and murmured, 'Named after her mother—Adeline.'

'I beg your pardon?' Adelina was becoming tired of being the subject of their musings which she could not understand. Impatiently, she said, 'I've come from America to find my grandfather. My parents are dead and...'

The old lady gasped and Lord Lynwood twisted round to face Adelina. 'What?' they both cried together.

Adelina looked from one shocked face to the other.

'Er—m-my parents are—dead,' she repeated.

Lynwood gave a groan and sank down into a chair. His face turned a deathly white. As for Lady Lynwood, she seemed to accept Adelina's news more calmly, but there was a sadness in her eyes that had not been there a few moments ago.

'You'd better ride to Abbeyford Grange and see Lord Royston, Francis,' Lady Lynwood murmured, her gaze still upon Adelina. 'Tell him—tell him what has happened and...' She paused and directed her question at Adelina. 'When—and how—did your mother die?'

'About ten years ago,' was Adelina's husky reply. 'In childbirth. The baby died too.'

'And your father?' There was gentleness in Lady Lynwood's tone.

'Just before I came to England.' Adelina lowered her head, not wanting to tell them the sordid details of her recent life, of her father's death. Thinking her reluctance to say more stemmed from the newness of her grief, Lady Lynwood probed no further.

'Go to Abbeyford, Francis, and see him,' she told her son.

'I'm sorry,' Lord Lynwood told Adelina on his return from Abbeyford. 'But—Lord Royston cannot bring himself to see you.' Pain flickered briefly in Lynwood's own eyes, as if he understood her grandfather's feelings only too well.

Adelina said, 'May I ask why not?'

Lynwood's shoulders lifted fractionally. 'He has not forgiven your mother, I suppose.'

'Forgiven her? What for?'

He looked at her then, fully. 'Don't you know what happened here twenty years ago?'

Adelina almost laughed, but the hurt in his eyes stopped her. 'I didn't even know of Lord Royston's existence until a few months ago. I found this locket.'

She opened the locket at her throat and Lynwood bent forward. The miniatures were faded but still recognisable. He straightened up.

'Lord Royston gave that to his daughter—your mother. He held a grand ball at Abbeyford Grange in honour of Guy Trent's marriage, but, in the midst of it, she slipped away and eloped with the bailiff on the estate—one Thomas Cole!' The bitterness was back in his tone. 'I presume he was your father, since you bear the same name.'

Adelina nodded.

'Afterwards—Lord Royston became a recluse. He never forgave them. Nor does he want to see you now!'

'I see.' Sadly, Adelina turned away.

'But he's not a vindictive man. He realises that what happened is no fault of yours,' Lynwood was saying, whilst Adelina waited, her back still towards him, her head lowered. 'He has asked me to see Martha Langley—Caroline's cousin—to see if she will take you in. Her husband is the Reverend Hugh Langley, Vicar of Abbeyford. They live at Abbeyford Vicarage.'

Adelina twisted round, her green eyes flashing. 'I don't want charity!' she snapped. 'I can take care of myself.

I've done it for the past few years...' The words were out before she could prevent them.

Lynwood's eyebrows lifted fractionally, but he did not question her. One glance at her clothing told him that life could not have been one of ease and comfort for her.

'Give Lord Royston time. My news was a shock. He may—I'm not saying he will—but if he knows you're close at hand still, he may relent.' Lynwood smiled. 'His curiosity to see his only grandchild may work in your favour, Miss Cole.'

'Very well, but only for a short time. I'll not stay where I'm not wanted,' she told him determinedly.

'I don't see why we must take her in,' Martha Langley muttered as her own daughter, Emily, ushered their unexpected guest from the room and took her upstairs.

'Oh, come now, Martha my dear,' Hugh said. 'It was a shock for you, I know, seeing her and so like your poor, dear cousin.'

'"Poor, dear cousin," my foot!' countered Martha. 'I'll not deny her daughter's sudden arrival out of the blue has caused me considerable unease. But not,' she added vehemently, 'in the way you mean.'

Leaning towards her husband, she said, 'You realise what this means, don't you?'

Agitated, Hugh Langley clasped and unclasped his womanish hands. 'I—I don't understand you, Martha.'

'She's a threat to Emily's inheritance. *That's* what I mean!'

Hugh Langley looked shocked. 'Martha —how can you think of that when the poor child is a homeless orphan? I would not have thought you so uncharitable.' It was the closest he ever came to remonstrating with his wife.

'Uncharitable? It'll be a sight more than "charity" if *she* inherits from Lord Royston now, instead of our own daughter!' Martha Langley said tartly.

Mr Langley shook his head sadly. He'd tried, oh how he'd tried over the years to soften Martha's mercenary streak, her bitterness against her wealthier relations. Then, after Caroline's elopement and the birth of their own daughter, Emily, Lord Royston had altered his Will and had made no secret of the fact that he had cut out his own wayward daughter and had made baby Emily Langley heiress to his entire estate.

Martha's vindictiveness had been mellowed somewhat by his action. But now, threatened again by the arrival of Caroline's daughter—Lord Royston's own granddaughter, a close blood relative whereas Emily was only distantly connected to him and that by marriage—all Martha Langley's jealousy was rekindled.

Emily led Adelina up the stairs and along the dark landing to a room at the rear of the Vicarage.

'This,' she said, sounding almost apologetic as she opened the door, 'is your room.'

Adelina stepped inside. To anyone else the bedroom would have appeared poorly furnished. There was a high, hard single bed, a dressing-table and wash-stand and a tall, narrow wardrobe. The bedspread was obviously old and patched here and there, and the faded blue curtains scarcely covered the window. But to Adelina, who had more than once slept on bare boards with only one moth-eaten blanket as a cover, it was comfort indeed!

'There's some water in the ewer and clean towels nearby,' Emily said. 'I'll leave you to freshen up. Please,' she begged, lacing her fingers together nervously, 'don't be too long. Dinner will be served very soon, and Mama dislikes unpunctuality.' Then she gave Adelina a quick, hesitant smile and left the room.

Adelina went over to the window. Immediately below her window was part of the Vicarage garden and the village green, then the road and a row of cottages. Behind them was a strip of meadow-land and the stream and then the ground rose. Adelina's gaze travelled up the hill until she saw a mansion standing just below the top of the hill.

'That must be Abbeyford Grange,' she murmured, 'where Lord Royston lives.' She found it impossible to think of him as her grandfather. He was only a remote image created in her mind. Sadly she turned from the window and left the bedroom. Emily was waiting for her in the hall.

The meal was passed in an uncomfortable silence. Covertly, Adelina appraised her new-found relatives. Martha Langley sat stiffly at one end of the dining-table. She was thin with angular features, a pointed chin, a long nose and narrow, almost non-existent lips. At the opposite end of the table, Mr Langley stooped over his plate, his shoulders permanently rounded. He was bald except for tufts of wispy white hair over his ears. His manner was diffident, rather fussy, and yet Adelina could sense his kindliness towards her.

Emily, seated opposite Adelina, was small and slim, but rather plain. Her brown hair was pulled tightly back from her face into a coil. Her dress—though of good material and well-made—was a drab grey.

At any moment Adelina expected to be questioned about her parents, but Martha Langley remained obstinately tight-lipped and silent.

After casting several glances towards his wife, and then sighing softly to himself, Mr Langley turned to Adelina and said, 'What happened to your mother, my dear?'

Martha Langley's head snapped up, but resolutely he ignored his wife. 'And your father?'

'My mother died ten years ago, in childbirth—the baby too. My father...' she hesitated, reluctant to be disloyal to her father, yet she could not hide the truth for ever. 'My father,' she continued firmly, 'suffered much after her death. He never fully recovered. Eventually, we lost everything. He—he died shortly before I came to England.'

'So,' Martha put in waspishly, 'you thought you'd look up your wealthy relative, did you?'

'Martha!' Mr Langley's tone was gently warning, but his wife would not be silenced.

'Well, let me tell you, my girl, Emily is Lord Royston's heiress and nothing and no one is going to change that!'

Emily blushed scarlet and hung her head, whilst Adelina's own heightened colour came from an indignant anger. She sprang to her feet, the chair falling backwards with a crash at the violence of her sudden movement. She faced Martha Langley squarely. 'If I'm not welcome by my mother's own folk, I'll go—at once!' Impetuously, she made as if to turn and leave the room and the house that very instant.

Mr Langley's soothing voice spoke up. 'Adelina, Adelina. Sit down, child, do. You shall stay with us for a short while, until his lordship has had time to—to make up his mind. This has all been a great shock for us, my dear, you must realise that.'

Adelina saw him glance at his wife again. 'We were not even aware of your existence, nor of your mother's death. You must give us all time to adjust to the situation.'

Anger still smouldered in Adelina's green eyes. 'I'm not a fortune-hunter, if that is what you are thinking,' she declared.

'No, no, my dear, of course you are not.' Once again the gentle eyes were directed at Martha, but with a note of firmness in his tone now, he added, 'You shall stay here until after Christmas at least. Then we shall see what is to be done.'

Martha Langley shot him a look of malice, her thin lips tight, but she said no more.

Later, alone in her room, after she had undressed down to her chemise, Adelina went over to the window and opened it. She leaned out and breathed the night air deeply. Her fingers touched the leaves of an ivy tree which covered the outside wall and wound itself round her window. High up on the hill she could see Abbeyford Grange where her grandfather, Lord Royston, lived in lonely splendour.

If only she could see him, could meet him, just once. She touched the locket around her neck, her fingers tracing the ruby set in the centre and the smaller diamonds surrounding it. As she gazed through the darkness at the house her mother had once called home, Adelina felt the yearning to belong—really belong—to someone. She resolved that somehow she would find a way of meeting her grandfather—no matter who stood in her way!

CHAPTER 3

The following day Emily took Adelina for a walk to show her the village.

Abbeyford lay in its own shallow valley in gently rolling countryside some fifteen miles south of Manchester. In the centre of the village was the church and the Vicarage, the green and the duckpond, and clustering around them were the villagers' cottages. On the hill-slope to the east, just below the summit, stood the half-timbered Grange, built in the Tudor style. On the opposite hillside was Abbeyford Manor, a square, solid house with stables to one side and farm buildings at the rear. Above the Manor and a little to the south, on the very top of the hill, the abbey ruins rose gaunt and black against the sky.

From the waterfall where Adelina had first met Lord Lynwood, a stream ran through the wood, channelling a deep gully, down the hill and into the valley and on through the common. The lane leading from the village up to the Manor ran through this stream, literally, for there was only a narrow footbridge across the water at this point. Farm-carts and the gentry's carriages had to splash through the ford in the lane. Another stream ran from the eastern hillside through the valley and at the southern end the two streams joined together and ran as one out of the valley through a natural pass between the hills to join a river some miles away.

The two girls looked in the church with its grey stone and shining wooden pews and then walked across the green. A few children played in the roadway and here and there a woman sat in her doorway spinning. Adelina was shocked to see that the children ran barefoot and that their clothes were ragged and dirty. The low, squat cottages, too, were tumble-down.

Doors hung off their hinges and broken windows were stuffed with sackcloth to keep out the cold.

Emily linked her arm through Adelina's. 'I'm glad you've come, Adelina. I hope we shall be friends.'

After Mrs Langley's open hostility, Emily's gesture was all the more surprising. 'I've to take a message to Mrs Smithson,' Emily said. 'She helps out at the Vicarage sometimes.'

She stepped towards one of the cottages and knocked upon the door. It was opened, somewhat tentatively Adelina thought, by a woman.

'Mrs Smithson, I have a message from my mother...' The woman's stare travelled past Emily and saw Adelina. 'Oh, this is Miss Adelina Cole. She's from America. Our mothers were cousins, you know.'

The woman's eyes widened as she looked at Adelina. Then she gasped and one hand fluttered nervously to her throat while the other gripped the door fiercely as if to gain support.

'What is it, Mrs Smithson?' Emily asked. 'Are you ill?'

'No, no. But it's like seein' a ghost, miss.' She continued to gaze at Adelina.

'You mean Adelina is like her mother? Yes, Mama, was saying so.'

'I can scarce believe it, Miss Emily!'

'Mrs Smithson, Mama says can you come to the Vicarage tomorrow afternoon?'

The woman nodded absently, hardly seeming to hear Emily, her attention still upon Adelina.

Sarah Smithson must once have been very pretty, beautiful in a natural way, Adelina supposed, but now she wore the lines of defeat and bitterness upon her tired face. Her mouth was drawn into a tight line, her shoulders drooping, and her movements were slow and lethargic as if life held little interest or meaning for her. She was dressed in a shapeless blouse and a coarse brown skirt. Her eyes were dull and sorrowful and her hair, once black and shining, was now grey.

Sarah Smithson blinked and seemed to recover her senses. 'What—oh, yes, I'll be there, miss.'

As Emily and Adelina walked back to the Vicarage they passed several villagers. Each one smiled and bade Emily 'good-day'. Then their eyes strayed to the stranger at her side. Their reactions were varied. A young girl merely smiled and passed on. A youth grinned cheekily, his admiration of Adelina apparent. But two older women, walking together, stared at Adelina with open astonishment, and as they passed by they whispered to each other.

'It seems,' Adelina remarked, 'that my appearance has a strange effect upon some of the villagers.'

'The older ones—yes. Those who remember seeing your mother. Mama says your likeness to your mother is uncanny.'

Adelina was silent. Just what could her mother have done to arouse such deep resentment that it had lasted all these years? First Lord Lynwood, then Martha Langley—and of course Lord Royston, who would not even meet his own granddaughter!

They walked on. Adelina asked suddenly, 'Lord Royston—he owns all this?' She waved her hand to encompass not only the farmland on the surrounding hillsides and the cattle grazing there, but the tumbledown cottages too.

'Why—yes.' Emily turned her wide eyes upon Adelina. 'Why do you ask?'

'I just wondered why he doesn't do a little more for his tenants?'

Emily blushed. 'Lord Royston has nothing

to do with the day to day running of his estate.'

'Then who has?' Adelina demanded sharply, growing more disgusted at the poverty she saw where there was no reason for the people to be so poor.

'The Trents. I suppose Wallis Trent really, since his father, Squire Guy Trent,' she paused as if searching for the right words, 'takes little active part in running the estate.'

'Hmm, I should like to meet this—Wallis Trent,' Adelina murmured.

'You'll meet him tomorrow night,' Emily was saying softly.

Adelina turned to look at her. Emily's face wore a dreamy expression and two bright pink spots of colour burned in her cheeks.

'Will I indeed? How?'

'He'll be dining with us tomorrow evening.' Emily spoke reverently. Adelina raised her left eyebrow in surprise, but asked no more questions.

The following evening, Adelina viewed her one gown critically. The old skirt she had worn before was beyond salvation, but now the dress the tinker had given her seemed tawdry beside Emily's neat, finely stitched gowns. Adelina sighed and pursed her lips grimly as she pulled it over her head. She refused to give Martha Langley the satisfaction of hearing her ask for anything. She would sooner wear this one dress until it fell from her back! Adelina thought.

She was very soon ready. She knocked on Emily's door and entered. As she turned from her dressing-table, Emily appeared prettier than usual. There was the light of happiness shining in her eyes, a rosy blush to her cheeks. Her gown, though plain and demure, was of good material and fitted her slim figure well. Her soft brown hair shone.

'Oh, Adelina—haven't you any other gown but that one? Oh I'm sorry,' she added swiftly. 'I didn't mean to hurt your feelings.'

Adelina smiled ruefully.

'I expect you lost all your clothes on the voyage, did you?' Adelina did not contradict Emily's kindly invention and the girl hurried on, 'If it won't offend you—there—there are one or two of my gowns we might alter to fit you, though you are a little more—shapely than me.' There was a wistful note in Emily's voice.

Despite the poor, faded gown, Adelina was still strikingly lovely with her clear skin, auburn hair and green eyes. Adelina smiled. Emily's offer held none of the resentment her mother harboured.

'Thank you, Emily. That would be sweet of you.'

Wallis Trent rose from the sofa as the two girls entered the drawing-room. He was, Adelina thought, the tallest man she had ever seen. His hair was jet black and his eyes grey. His presence seemed to fill the room. There was an aura of power and authority about him.

Mrs Langley made the introductions grudgingly. 'This is a distant cousin, Wallis.' There was a distinct accent upon the description 'distant', but there was a fleeting surprise in Wallis's cool eyes, quickly hidden. He took Adelina's hand in his and his voice as he greeted her was deep but lacked warmth.

During the evening Adelina found herself studying Wallis Trent. She noticed every tiny detail about him—a fine-cut tailcoat and a frilled shirt beneath a low-cut waistcoat. His hair was short, but, unlike Lord Lynwood's, without a trace of curl.

At the dinner-table, the Reverend Mr Langley and Mrs Langley sat at either end while two places for Wallis and Emily had been set on one side with one place opposite for Adelina.

Wallis Trent, seated on the right hand of the Vicar, turned to him for conversation. 'How is your historical research on the Amberly family progressing, sir?' He asked politely during the soup course.

'Oh, admirably, my boy. It really is fascinating. I'm sure you would be interested. Lord Lynwood's family have a fine record, you know. Oh, of course, there have been a few black sheep...'

Was it Adelina's imagination that she saw Wallis's jaw harden at his words? Perhaps not, for Mr Langley himself seemed suddenly embarrassed and hurried on swiftly.

'A-hem! Did you know that one of Francis's uncles, his father's younger brother, fought with Cornwallis in the War of American Independence? Why, Adelina, my dear, this would interest you. He was killed in Yorktown, just before the final surrender.'

Adelina smiled but she had little knowledge of the subject. Her fight had been for mere survival. She had had no time to worry about the wars and battles of history. But she did not wish to appear ignorant, so she listened intently, and said, 'You mean Lord Lynwood's uncle?'

'Yes, my dear,' Mr Langley replied.

'You know Lord Lynwood?' There was surprise in Wallis Trent's tone and she could feel his eyes upon her dowdy gown.

'Yes—I—er—met him when I arrived here.'

'Are you staying here long, Miss Adelina?'

'I—don't quite...'

Mrs Langley interrupted. 'Adelina must find employment. Her parents are dead.'

There was an awkward silence around the dinner-table. It was as if Wallis Trent were waiting for Mrs Langley—or someone—to tell him more about Adelina, and Mrs Langley's short, clipped sentences gave the impression that there was certainly more to tell, but that she had no intention of telling it.

'I see...' Wallis murmured, but his tone implied that he did not.

Then a thought came to Adelina. Wallis Trent was her grandfather's tenant-farmer. Perhaps he was on friendly terms with Lord Royston. Perhaps a man like Wallis

Trent, with his authoritative manner, could help her. Impetuously, she said, 'I thought perhaps, that if only—I could meet my grandfather...'

'Be quiet, Adelina,' Mrs Langley snapped.

Wallis glanced quickly at Mrs Langley and frowned slightly. Ignoring her command he addressed Adelina. 'Your grandfather, Miss Adelina? And who might that be?'

Everyone was motionless, the silence tense and watchful.

Adelina hesitated. She realised she had spoken out hastily, but it was too late to draw back now.

'Lord Royston.'

'Lord Royston!' Wallis repeated, his frown deepening noticeably. 'I see,' he added slowly, this time with more obvious understanding.

'Lord Royston does not acknowledge her as his granddaughter,' Mrs Langley said pointedly. 'He disowned her mother twenty years ago when she eloped with the bailiff of the estate.'

'But you're hoping your grandfather might relent now, are you?' Wallis was still speaking directly to Adelina.

'I only—wanted to meet him. To—to

see where my mother had lived. Is that so very wrong?'

Wallis shook his head. 'No—no I suppose not. If that is all you *do* want.'

The meal was finished amidst embarrassed silence, and conversation in the drawing-room afterwards was stilted and strained. Wallis Trent appeared to be thoughtful, as if deliberating with cool calculation, and often Adelina could feel his gaze upon her.

As he took his leave, he turned to Adelina and, smiling now, asked, 'Do you ride, Miss Adelina?'

'I...' she hesitated. She had not, of course, ridden for a long time and yet, hazily, she seemed to remember having done so as a child.

Boldly she answered, 'Yes, yes, of course.'

'Then my stables are at your disposal. I should deem it an honour to take you riding and show you the countryside.'

She heard Mrs Langley's swift intake of breath and a gasp from Emily.

'Why, thank you, Mr Trent,' Adelina replied politely. 'That—that would be most kind of you.'

He took her hand and kissed it. Then

he said 'goodnight' to the others and was gone.

As soon as the front door closed behind him, Emily burst into tears and fled upstairs to her room. Bewildered, Adelina turned to meet the hostile eyes of Martha Langley. There was hatred in the woman's expression and, strangely, a look of fear. 'Why did you have to come here?' she hissed.

'I—don't understand why Emily is so upset?'

Mrs Langley thrust her thin, angular face close to Adelina and said, 'Emily is betrothed to Wallis Trent.'

'What has that to do with me?' Adelina asked.

'Nothing—and everything!' was Martha Langley's puzzling reply.

The next morning, Sunday, Adelina, heavy-eyed, found herself being aroused even earlier than usual.

'You've to go to early service at the church, miss,' the housemaid explained, 'with the mistress and Miss Emily. They always go.'

Adelina groaned but roused herself.

Much to her surprise she found that the

bright, clear morning air invigorated her. The dew was still on the grass and the birds twittered in the trees and hedgerows.

Adelina found herself the centre of attention even amongst the devout few who attended such an early service. No doubt, she thought wryly, word of her arrival would have passed round and those who remembered her mother would have revived all the old scandal and gossip.

As they returned home together, Adelina tried to draw Emily from her quiet mood. The girl's eyes were red with weeping and her mouth still trembled, but she uttered no word of reproach to Adelina.

'There weren't many in church, Emily.'

'No—it's very early. Matins and Evensong are better attended, you'll see.'

Adelina stopped and turned to face her. 'Do you mean we have to go again today?'

'Why, of course.'

'To *both* services?'

'Yes. That's what the Sabbath is for,' Emily said primly. 'Besides, it brings the whole village together in an act of worship right from the Squire of the Manor down to the labourers and their families.'

'Does—does Lord Royston attend church?'

Adelina asked hesitantly.

'No,' Emily replied with uncharacteristic harshness in her voice. Then she sighed and, in a rush of tender feeling towards Adelina, put her hand upon her arm. 'I wish you would forget the idea of meeting your grandfather. He has said he does not want to see you, and—and...'

'Yes?' Adelina prompted.

'And my mother will see to it that you don't meet him!'

'I see,' Adelina murmured, her tone flat with disappointment. 'So everyone is against me.'

Emily did not answer.

Evensong, as Emily had predicted, was far better attended than the earlier services. Mrs Langley, Emily and Adelina were already settled in their pew when Wallis Trent entered the church with his mother on his arm. As they took their place in the Trent family box pew, Adelina was aware of the glances and whisperings exchanged amongst the villagers. She was surprised, after what Emily had implied, that there were no smiles of welcome for their employer and his mother, their faces were resentful. Instead of uniting employer and employee it was as if they felt the Trents had intruded upon their one social event of the week.

Lady Louisa Trent was a tall, stately woman. Once she must have been very beautiful, with a flawless skin and grey eyes, but time and life had etched bitterness into her face. Her mouth was tight and unsmiling, and her eyes held some deep sadness. She was dressed in a pale blue pelisse trimmed with braid and tassles. She carried a matching reticule and parasol and her bonnet was trimmed with a darker shade of blue velvet ribbon.

Suddenly a hushed whisper and a stir ran through the congregation, and the few who dared, turned to see Lord Lynwood enter the church with his mother, the Dowager Countess of Lynwood.

The Earl glanced from side to side as he progressed slowly up the aisle, the Countess leaning heavily on a stick in her left hand and with her right arm through her son's. He appeared to be looking for someone.

Then the Earl saw Adelina and his eyes stopped their restless roaming. He smiled slowly at her and Adelina smiled in return, suddenly realising how very glad she was to see him again.

The Earl and Lady Lynwood took their places in a box pew on the opposite side of the aisle to the Trents, to whom they nodded in greeting.

Once more, Lady Lynwood was dressed entirely in black, her hat giving the only relief to her sombre outfit, being topped with three large white plumes, and the crown encircled by a white ribbon and bow.

Throughout the service, Adelina was acutely aware of the presence of both Lord Lynwood and Wallis Trent. They stood in front of her, tall and straight, Wallis a head taller than the slim and elegant Earl.

The service ended and the Earl and his mother left the church first, followed by the Trents. There was much reluctant curtsying and forelock-touching from the village folk, but at last Mrs Langley, Emily and Adelina were able to leave. Outside, the Dowager Countess was waiting.

'Mrs Langley.' Her ladyship's voice rang out. Adelina was amused to see the haughty Martha Langley obliged to curtsy to her superior. 'You're looking well,' Lady

Lynwood said and then her sharp eyes fell upon Adelina. 'Ah, Miss Adelina, we meet again.' Her eyes, twinkling with mischief, met Adelina's. Then Lady Lynwood gave her strange cackle of laughter, and pointed her stick at Adelina with a sharp prodding movement.

'You'll have your work cut out with this one, Martha Langley. She'll not be as docile as your own little foal. *She's too much like her mother!*'

Mrs Langley's mouth pursed and the fingers of her hands clenched. Adelina guessed that Mrs Langley would dearly love to answer the old lady with some sharp retort, but dared not.

'Come and visit me, Miss Adelina, whenever you wish. You're a girl with spirit—I like that. Your mother used to visit me often—it'll be like old times.' She nodded, turned and once more leaning heavily on Lord Lynwood's arm, she moved towards her carriage. Adelina saw Lynwood bend towards his mother as he helped her into the carriage and say something to her. Again Lady Lynwood's cackling laugh rang out, then she patted her son on the arm and glanced across at Adelina and nodded knowingly. The Earl did not climb into the carriage, but closed the door and bade the coachman 'drive on' to leave him standing on the roadside.

Lady Trent, too, stepped into her carriage alone, Wallis remaining at Emily's side.

Lord Lynwood was standing before Adelina. 'Miss Cole.' He bowed towards her but there was mockery in his action. Not to be outdone, Adelina curtsied pertly. 'My lord.'

'I have seen your grandfather this morning.' Concern for her and some hidden pain seemed to be fighting for control of his features. 'But he is still of the same mind.'

'It was kind of you to try,' she smiled up at him.

His eyes searched her face, boring into her soul, but he did not return her smile.

'You're so incredibly like her,' he murmured. 'It's hard to believe...'

Adelina sighed. 'But I am *not* her. I am Adelina.'

For an instant his face cleared of his inner anguish and she glimpsed how differently he—and everyone else—might treat her if she were not the living image of her mother.

'Yes, yes, of course you are.' He smiled and his face became suddenly more boyish, more roguishly handsome. He held out his arm to her. 'May I escort you home, Miss Cole?'

She was about to accept his offer graciously when Wallis Trent approached them. The two men nodded curtly to each other, and Wallis said to Adelina, 'Mrs Langley has asked me to escort you and Emily to the Vicarage.'

Adelina almost laughed aloud. How foolish all this was! Why, here were two men exchanging hostile looks over who was to escort her home, when the Vicarage was only a few yards away, right next to the church. It was ridiculous!

Lord Lynwood dropped his arm and the brooding expression was back in his eyes. 'I'll bid you "goodnight" then, Miss Cole,' he said tersely and without meeting her gaze again, he strode away. Adelina watched him go, wondering at his strange, erratic changes of mood.

'...If you are free tomorrow,' Wallis Trent was saying.

'I'm sorry. What did you say?' Adelina dragged her attention from Lord Lynwood's disappearing figure to concentrate on what Mr Trent had been saying.

'I said, "I should be happy to take you riding if you are free tomorrow." '

'Oh—I—er, yes, thank you. And Emily too?'

The smile faded a little from Wallis Trent's face. 'Of course, if she wishes to come. But I thought she did not ride.'

'I—don't know. I haven't asked her.'

At that moment Emily moved towards them and with a determined cheerfulness stepped between them and linked her arms through theirs. So, with Wallis on her left arm and Adelina on her right, Emily drew them down the narrow churchyard path towards the Vicarage.

Wallis and Adelina walked in silence and, though Emily chattered about the weather, her father's sermon and the presence of the Earl of Lynwood and his mother, it was with a forced gaiety, a pretence that nothing was wrong.

'It's unusual for them to come to our church, isn't it, Wallis? The Dowager Countess is wonderful, though I must admit to being a little afraid of her. They say she was a great beauty in her day and had all the gentlemen falling at her—her feet!' There was a catch in her voice as if the longing to be beautiful herself was too much to bear.

As they reached the Vicarage gate, Wallis said, 'I shall expect you at the Manor at three tomorrow afternoon, Emily. I shall take Adelina riding. You may come with us, if you wish,' his tone was uninviting, 'or stay and talk to my mother. She's always glad to see you.'

'Yes, Wallis,' Emily said meekly.

He gave a small bow. 'I'll say "good-night", then.' And he was gone.

Three o'clock the following afternoon found the two girls walking up the lane towards Abbeyford Manor. Adelina was dressed in a riding-habit borrowed from the tight-lipped Martha Langley, who would have liked to have refused but dare not, since it was Wallis Trent who had issued the invitation. The habit must be twenty years old, Adelina thought, and it was far too tight for her figure, but at least it was a riding-habit. Emily walked beside her in silence. They crossed the wooden footbridge near the ford and took the left-hand fork in the lane towards the Manor. Emily led the way through a small gate from the lane directly into the stableyard so that they did not go near the front of the house.

Suddenly, Emily stopped, her eyes widening and her cheeks blushing furiously. 'Oh dear!' she whispered.

'What is it?' Adelina, who had walked a few paces ahead, stopped too and turned to look back at Emily. Then she followed the line of Emily's wide-eyed gaze and saw a man walking the distance of the hundred yards or so from the house to the stable and slapping his riding-boots with his whip as he walked. Adelina's eyes narrowed as she took in his appearance, and at Emily's whisper, 'It's Squire Trent—Wallis's father!' Adelina watched him with interest. He was rather small for a man, but stocky and powerfully built. His head was bare and showed a fine head of hair, still red though slightly greying at the temples.

Squire Trent, Adelina noticed, still wore breeches and top-boots, though these were now no longer worn by the younger men of fashion. His blue eyes were dull and bloodshot, his teeth yellow and broken.

As he saw the two girls, he stopped and blinked as if he thought they were some drink-induced mirage.

'My God!' he muttered under his breath. 'Royston's daughter!' He blinked again and shook his head slightly as if trying to clear his muddled thoughts. 'No, no, it can't be! That was years ago.' He put his hand to his head. 'Who the devil *are* you?'

'I'm Adelina Cole. Lord Royston's *grand*daughter.'

He nodded slowly as realisation dawned upon him. 'There's no mistaking that. Dear God, but you're the image of her! It's as if... God, how you bring back the memories!'

Guy Trent, wavering a little unsteadily on his feet, gazed at Adelina's face, drinking in her loveliness and her youth. And as he did so the wasted years seemed to roll away and he could almost believe himself to be once more the virile, attractive, impulsive young man he had once been.

'Oh, there's Wallis,' Emily cried, relief evident in her tone, and Adelina looked up to see Wallis striding across the stableyard towards them, an angry frown upon his face.

Squire Trent gave a grunt, winked broadly, though a little tipsily, at Adelina. 'I'd better be on my way if my sobersides son is about to descend upon us.' He sighed dramatically. 'He always seems to spoil my fun.' His voice dropped to a whisper and he leant closer to Adelina, his breath hot and evil-smelling upon her face. 'I do hope we meet again, Miss Cole.' With that he turned and walked unsteadily away towards a stable-lad holding a horse by its bridle. He waved his hand to his son. 'Just going, my boy, just going.'

A moment later, Squire Trent rode out of the yard, looking none too safe on his mount, waving wildly to Adelina.

Why, she thought, he's afraid of his own son, and she felt a flash of pity for the drink-sodden, unhappy man who lived on his memories.

'Good afternoon, Miss Adelina—Emily,' Wallis greeted them.

'I will—go and see your mother, Wallis, if—that is convenient?'

'Of course, my dear,' Wallis smiled slightly. 'You'll find her on the terrace.'

'G-goodbye then, Adelina. Enjoy your ride.' She turned away swiftly as if to hide the tears.

The stable-boy was leading a horse forward to the mounting block.

'Ah, here is Stardust for you to ride, Adelina.'

Now that the moment had arrived, Adelina regretted her bravado. She moved towards the horse, biting her lip and trying to remember what she should do. But she need not have feared, for as soon as she stood upon the mounting block and felt the smooth leather of the saddle beneath her fingers and touched the horse's neck, the knowledge she must have learned in childhood came flooding back instinctively. She mounted quite easily and held the reins. It surprised Adelina herself to find that she knew exactly what to do without hesitation. For a moment the longing for the lost years of her childhood with both her mother and father, the happier years, threatened to engulf her. Then she saw Wallis mounting a magnificent animal, a wild-eyed stallion, his shining coat jet black.

'This is Jupiter,' Wallis called to her. 'Do you like him?'

'He's superb.'

Wallis patted the horse's neck, his action showing his pride in the possession of such an animal. 'Come, let us begin our ride.'

They left the stableyard and trotted up

the lane to the wood. Winding through the trees they came to the open fields on top of the hill. Wallis urged his horse to a steady canter and, feeling more confident now, Adelina did the same. They rode towards the abbey ruins, and when they came within the shadow of the crumbling walls they reined in.

Adelina looked up at the decaying building with interest. 'It's a lonely place,' she said and shuddered.

Wallis frowned. 'The villagers fear the place—some stupid superstition which I think has been put about by those who wish to use it for their own purposes.'

'Whatever could you use a place like this for?'

Wallis smiled a little. 'A trysting place, perhaps, for lovers to meet in secret.'

Adelina's eyes were drawn once more to the cold stones. Perhaps her mother and father had met in this very place all those years ago.

Suddenly there was a movement and the figure of a man appeared on one of the walls. He stood, his legs wide apart, his arms akimbo, looking down at them. The horses shied a little at the man's sudden appearance.

'What the devil are you doing here?' Wallis Trent shouted angrily. 'Why aren't you working?'

'Oh, I'm working, Mr Trent, I'm working.' His tone was insolent. 'One of the sheep strayed. I'm looking for her.'

Wallis snorted disbelievingly. 'Well, be about your work, then.'

The man made no move to obey, bitterness and hatred in his blue eyes as he looked down at Wallis Trent. He was stockily built, with broad shoulders and slim waist and hips. He wore a loose shirt, open to the waist and with the sleeves rolled up above his elbows, showing his tanned, muscular arms. Around his neck was knotted a red spotted neckcloth. He wore breeches with leather leggings buttoned on the outside of each leg from ankle to above his knee, and heavy boots. He had a shock of red hair and white, even teeth.

Adelina frowned slightly. He seemed to remind her vaguely of someone...

Wallis was speaking again. 'I said be about...'

The man sprang from the wall and leapt the small distance between himself and Wallis's horse. Jupiter reared, but the young man, showing no fear, caught hold of the bridle.

'Mr Trent—*sir...*' Instead of being a polite salutation, his tone was a sarcastic insult.

'Let go my horse,' Wallis Trent hissed between clenched teeth.

'When are you going to repair my mother's cottage, to say nothing of all the other cottages in the village? You treat your animals better than your workmen!'

'Leave hold my horse,' Wallis said with dangerous emphasis on every word.

The young man held on, his face turned up towards Wallis. 'When you've answered my question—*sir!*'

Adelina saw Wallis raise his riding-crop, and a small scream escaped her lips as he brought it down with a single vicious stroke across the man's face. The man winced and turned his face away but, to her surprise, Adelina saw that he still held the bridle fast in his hand.

'Aye, you'd like to kill me, wouldn't you?' his voice was low and menacing and then he added but one more word, putting into it every ounce of the hatred that was in his heart. 'Wouldn't you, *brother?*'

Then he let go of the horse, turned and

walked away but not before Adelina had seen the purple weal made by Wallis's whip swelling on his cheek. She stared after him and as she did so the thought came to her that he was the first person she had met in Abbeyford who had no fear of Wallis Trent.

'Come,' Wallis was saying, breathing heavily with ill-concealed anger. 'We must return home.'

'Who—was that?'

There was a pause before Wallis replied. 'Evan Smithson. One of my employees, who seeks to rise above his station.' Then he urged his horse ahead as if to prevent Adelina asking further, unwelcoming questions.

CHAPTER 4

'Emily, who is Evan Smithson? Is he Sarah Smithson's son?'

'Oh, Adelina,' Emily said, her eyes wide with fear. 'You shouldn't be here. Mama will be angry. Go back to bed.'

After she had undressed in her own room

that night, Adelina had quietly unlatched her door, listened a moment to be sure there were no sounds coming from the lower rooms, and had crept along the landing to Emily's room.

Now she perched herself on the end of Emily's bed. 'Not until you've answered my questions,' she whispered.

Emily sighed. 'Oh very well. Yes—he's Sarah Smithson's son.'

'We met him this afternoon—up near the abbey ruins. Emily—he—he seems to hate Wallis? Why should that be?'

'I suppose he thinks he has good reason. He's—he's Squire Guy Trent's illegitimate son.'

Adelina gasped. 'Of course! The likeness is there. Why ever didn't I see it? But—surely, he's about the same age as Wallis, isn't he?'

Emily nodded. 'A year older, actually. Years ago, Guy Trent was as handsome and—and attractive as Evan is now. As you've seen, though, he drinks now and—and gambles...'

'But what about Evan? I mean—how...?'

'As a young man Guy was wild and irresistible. They say no girl was safe! He fell in love with a village girl—Sarah

Miller. She—she had his child, but neither her family nor his would let them marry.'

'What happened?'

'The Miller family arranged for Sarah to marry a distant cousin, Henry Smithson. But their life together has not been happy. Henry Smithson bears a grudge, and so now does Evan, against the Trent family.'

'Yes,' Adelina said slowly. 'Yes, I guess they do. And what about Guy Trent?'

'He married Louisa Marchant, the daughter of a wealthy clothing manufacturer from Manchester way, according to *his* parents' wishes. You saw her in church.'

'She didn't look exactly happy either,' Adelina remarked. 'But Wallis is their son, I take it?'

Emily nodded and seemed about to say more, but at that moment they both heard the stairs creak and Mrs Langley's familiar sniff.

'Oh Adelina,' Emily whispered frantically. 'We're caught. She always comes in here when she comes to bed.'

'Hush,' Adelina swung her feet to the floor. 'Lie down, Emily, and pretend to be asleep.' So saying Adelina lay on the floor and rolled under the bed. The coverlet fell down at the side to hide her completely. The latch lifted on the door and Mrs Langley whispered softly, 'Emily?' But when, after a moment, there was no reply from her daughter except her steady breathing, Mrs Langley closed the door again. When she heard the other bedroom door close too, Adelina rolled out from beneath the bed, stifling her helpless laughter. She scrambled to her feet and not trusting herself to speak to Emily, for she knew she would laugh aloud, Adelina escaped back to her own room. She jumped into bed and pulled the covers over her head as her merriment shook her.

Adelina surmised that perhaps Wallis Trent, who seemed to wield such power in Abbeyford valley, since neither Lord Royston nor his own father took much interest in the estate, might succeed where Lord Lynwood had failed.

She made up her mind that she would ask him to approach Lord Royston on her behalf.

'One last try,' Adelina told herself as she mounted Stardust in the stableyard at the Manor, 'and if that doesn't work, I'll leave Abbeyford!'

A busy harvest-time had kept Wallis away from the Vicarage for some time, but he had left word that Miss Adelina was to be allowed to ride Stardust whenever she wished. Taking advantage of his offer, Adelina slipped away from the Vicarage one afternoon and went in search of Wallis Trent.

She turned in the direction of the abbey, thinking that from such a vantage-point she would be able to see the workmen in the fields and perhaps see Wallis. As she drew near the ruins she could see plainly the gaunt walls, half gone, rising up grotesquely against the grey sky. It was a stark and lonely place and yet it fascinated Adelina, for she believed that perhaps her mother and father had met here when their love had to be kept a secret. She was surprised to see how much of the building was still standing as she walked into the ruins. Within the outer shell there were numerous other walls, in various stages of collapse. There was a large, oblong-shaped room which had perhaps been the refectory, narrow passages, smaller rooms which might have served as kitchens, then tiny cell-like rooms which must have been the monks' sleeping cells. One of these—the only one—still had its roof so that, inside the tiny square room, it was almost as it must have been before the abbey had been destroyed. Adelina stepped inside. The stone floor was remarkably clean—almost as if someone had swept it. The tiny slit of a window let in little light so that the cold stone room was dark and dismal and eerie. Adelina shuddered. Fancy spending one's entire life walled up in a tiny cell like this! She tried to look out of the narrow window, but it was too high.

'May I help, m'lady?'

Adelina jumped violently and a small scream escaped her lips as she spun round. She fell back against the wall, her hands spread against the rough stone. The figure of a man blocked the doorway, but she could not see his face clearly, merely his outline. He was only a little taller than she and thickset.

'You!' she gasped as she recognised Evan Smithson.

'Aye, 'tis me,' he answered and moved towards her. 'So you're Royston's granddaughter, are you? And you've wasted no time wi' me brother, I see. I've seen you ridin' round wi' 'im.'

'It's—not like that...'

Evan laughed hollowly. 'Expect me to believe that? You're a sight better lookin' than Miss Emily, I'll grant you that.' His eyes roved over her face and body. 'Aye, I've a fancy for you mesel'...'

At that moment there came the sound of footsteps over the loose stones which littered the floor of the ruins. Adelina ducked out of the small room and into the open again. Then a girl's voice rang eerily through the crumbling walls.

'Evan, Evan! You here, Evan?'

Adelina glanced back over her shoulder in amusement at the frowning young man. So, she thought, Evan Smithson used the abbey ruins as a trysting-place.

'Over here,' growled Evan, and a young girl appeared round the corner. She stopped uncertainly, her eyes widening in surprise as she saw Adelina. Adelina, too, was somewhat surprised herself, for the girl looked no more than fifteen or sixteen, though she gave every promise of womanhood. Long black hair fell about her shoulders like a cape and her coarse-woven dress was cut low at the neckline. Her face was thin and pinched, but her dark brown eyes flashed a look of jealousy plain for

Adelina to witness as they rested upon her, flickered briefly towards Evan, and then returned to Adelina to take in every detail of her appearance. The girl's hands, dirty and work-worn, plucked nervously at her brown skirt. Jealous she might be, for she had sense enough to recognise a worthy rival in Adelina, the mysterious beauty from a far-off land, of whom the villagers had gossiped never-endingly since the day of her arrival.

Evan grinned, suddenly, enjoying the spectacle of the two girls eyeing each other. The girl sidled closer to him until she stood beside him. Casually, he put his arm about her waist and drew her to him. The girl looked up at him adoringly, Adelina forgotten now. But Evan's eyes were still upon Adelina's face, challengingly.

Adelina's mouth curved and she threw back her head and laughed. 'I'll bid you "good-day", Mr Smithson.'

Lightly, she skipped over the rough ground and out of the ruins. Still laughing, she picked up the skirts of her borrowed riding-habit, mounted Stardust and cantered away.

Halfway down the hill, she saw Wallis riding Jupiter alongside the stream so she urged her mount forward. Seeing her, Wallis reined in and waited for her. He raised his hat and smiled as she neared him.

'Miss Adelina. What brings you out alone?'

Adelina reined in beside him. 'I was looking for you,' she replied with candour.

'I'm flattered.'

'I—want to ask you something.'

'Your wish is my command,' Wallis said pedantically.

'You seem to be a man of position around here,' Adelina began. 'I wondered if you would speak to my grandfather on my behalf. If—if you could persuade him to—to receive me.'

'Take you back into the family fold, you mean? Forgive and forget—everything.'

Adelina shook her head sadly. 'I can't expect him to forget, certainly. And—and I suppose he can't forgive, or he would have done so a long time ago. No, I just want to meet him. To know him. After all, he is my closest living relative now.'

'And you,' Wallis murmured thoughtfully, 'are *his* closest relative.'

They rode along side by side now and for some moments Wallis appeared deep in thought. Then he said slowly. 'I see your grandfather about once a month. I'll see what I can do.'

'Please—please will you speak to him the very next time you see him?'

Suddenly Wallis leaned over and to Adelina's surprise took hold of her hand. 'If I do, and he agrees to see you, then I may have a great deal to say to you concerning you and me.'

Then he let go of her hand, straightened up and turned away so swiftly that Adelina wondered if she had imagined his action and his words. Words which seemed almost a promise!

During the following weeks, Wallis's attentions towards Adelina became markedly more noticeable. He took her riding frequently and for carriage rides. All the while Emily's face became more forlorn and Mrs Langley's more outraged, but neither seemed to dare to speak out against Wallis Trent. Adelina felt trapped. She could not risk offending Wallis, for with him lay her last chance of a reconciliation with her grandfather.

Early in November, Mr Langley announced at breakfast that he was to visit Lynwood Hall that afternoon. 'I need to visit the library there to assist in my research. I have written to Lady Lynwood, asking her permission and she has graciously invited Adelina to take afternoon tea with her.'

'Why Adelina?' snapped Mrs Langley waspishly. 'Why not Emily?'

'I fancy her ladyship took a liking to Adelina, Martha my dear,' the Vicar replied mildly.

Martha Langley sniffed disapprovingly.

'You'd like to go, wouldn't you, Adelina?' Mr Langley was asking her.

Adelina hesitated momentarily, shaken by the sudden longing to see Lord Lynwood again. During the past few weeks she had scarcely thought of him, but now his every feature was suddenly, startlingly clear in her mind's eye. The brooding melancholy in his eyes, then the swift boyish smile that transformed his face. 'I would love to go, thank you.'

The carriage bowled along the lane out of Abbeyford, through Amberly and at last wound up the long drive towards Lynwood Hall through the parkland and drew to a halt before the house.

A liveried footman held open the door of the carriage for her to alight and another opened the heavy front door at the top of a flight of wide stone steps. Adelina stepped down from the carriage and daintily picked up her skirts to climb the steps into the hall.

The first time she had been here she had scarcely noticed her surroundings. Now Adelina saw that the interior was even more grand than the exterior. The oak floor was covered with Persian carpets. There were two staircases, with white balustrades, sweeping up on either side of the hall to join in a balcony at first-floor level. White busts of Amberly ancestors were set in alcoves, and the high white ceiling was dome-shaped.

'Welcome to Lynwood Hall,' a voice spoke softly behind her and Adelina turned to see Lord Lynwood leaning against a door-frame, his arms folded, a small smile of amusement upon his lips.

'My lord,' Adelina dropped a curtsy as she had seen the villagers do.

'Ah, there you are, my lord,' Mr Langley entered through the door at that moment. 'Your mama kindly asked Adelina to take tea with her whilst I peruse some of the documents in your fine library.'

Lord Lynwood inclined his head. 'Quite so, Mr Langley. Perhaps Miss Adelina will permit me to take her on a tour of Lynwood Hall before tea?'

The question was more a statement, for without waiting for either of them to reply, he offered Adelina his arm, his eyes never leaving her face, and when, shyly, she put her hand on his arm, he led her away leaving Mr Langley to find his own way to the library.

From the hall, Lord Lynwood took her through a seemingly endless number of rooms. Huge drawing-rooms with panelled walls, hung with tapestries, the dining-room with its long table with matching carved oak chairs, the walls almost covered with large oil paintings of the Amberly family. In the long gallery Adelina saw a portrait of Lady Lynwood, Francis's mother, as a young, beautiful woman with black shining hair and those same bright eyes which still twinkled with mischief in her now wrinkled face.

Room after room with painted ceilings, rich tapestries, priceless furniture and objects d'art. Adelina caught her breath as Lord Lynwood led her into the family's private chapel. Rows of high-backed chairs each with its own hassock. The altar was ornately carved out of white marble and rose almost to the ceiling, which was painted too. The lower half of each wall was panelled, but the upper half was entirely covered by a long mural running round the entire length of the chapel, depicting scenes from the Testaments.

'Oh, it's beautiful,' Adelina's husky whisper echoed eerily.

From there Lynwood led her through more rooms to a conservatory filled not only with plants of every conceivable kind but with more marble busts on pedestals.

'Well?' he asked, 'what do you think of my home, Adelina?'

'It's very beautiful,' Adelina repeated wistfully.

Today he seemed determined to charm her, to be the perfect host, but then his eyes clouded briefly. 'Your—your mother came here often.' With a supreme effort he brought his attention back to the present, to Adelina.

It was strange to have this girl here in his home, to see her sitting in the same chair where long ago Caroline had sat. She was so like her mother and yet there *was* a difference. In her eyes there was a depth of experience, of suffering, that Caroline in her protected world of luxury had never known. At least, Lynwood mused, not when he had known her. And there was a strength about Adelina too—a determination. Caroline, too, had been strong—ruthlessly, selfishly strong. Was Adelina so self-centred too? Lynwood didn't know. Part of him longed to find out, to test her, and yet he shied away from being hurt in the same way again. No woman, he had vowed, would ever have the power over him to inflict such hurt as Caroline had done—not even her beautiful, desirable daughter! And yet...

Adelina, intrigued by his lovely home, was acutely aware of Lynwood's swiftly changing moods, but could not begin to understand the cause.

A footman appeared. 'Her ladyship is waiting for the young lady, my lord.'

As Adelina turned to follow the footman she heard Lynwood, robbed of her company, swear softly under his breath.

After her visit to Lynwood Hall, Adelina passed the following days in a fever of hope. Soon now, Wallis Trent would surely see her grandfather. Every day she looked for him in the hope he would bring her news. Life within the Langley household was becoming unbearable.

Then one Sunday evening as Adelina and Emily left the shelter of the church porch and drew their capes closely about them against the flurry of light snow which had been falling since the afternoon, they found Wallis Trent suddenly beside them.

'Come, I'll see you home.' He stepped between them and offered each of them an arm.

'Oh, Wallis,' Emily breathed, looking up at him with adoring eyes. 'I didn't see you in church. I thought you had not come.'

'I was delayed earlier and could not arrive in time for the service, but I thought I might see you if I came now.'

Deliberately, it seemed, he avoided saying which of them he had come to see. There was a strained silence between the three of them as they walked the short distance from the church to the Vicarage, but on reaching the front door, Emily said, 'You will come in for a while, won't you, Wallis?'

He nodded. 'Of course, Emily.'

They found a warm log fire in the

dimly-lit drawing-room.

'I'll go and see about some hot chocolate for us,' Emily said with a forced cheerfulness. 'I won't be a moment.'

As the door closed, Wallis and Adelina, with one accord, turned towards each other.

'Have you seen him yet?' she asked eagerly.

'I went tonight, my dear, but I am afraid I was unable to broach the subject with him. He is a little unwell at the moment and—tetchy. I didn't think it wise to touch upon such a delicate matter.'

'Unwell?' Adelina asked worriedly. 'It's nothing serious, is it?'

Wallis's eyebrows rose fractionally. 'Why so concerned about someone you don't even know?'

'He's my grandfather. Of course I'm concerned. I want to meet him—to heal the breach, before it's too late.'

Wallis smiled and, sarcasm lining his words, replied, 'That I can well believe!'

'When will you see him again?'

'Shortly after Christmas.'

'Not before?'

'No. Listen, my dear, I'm sure you have no need to worry. I'm sure I shall be able to persuade him.' Wallis moved closer to take her hand in his. 'You are a beautiful woman, Adelina, and when things *are* settled between you and your grandfather, then...'

At that moment the door opened and Emily returned. Wallis and Adelina turned swiftly from each other, as guiltily as if they had been caught in a passionate embrace.

With shaking hands, Emily set the tray of cups upon the table, her cheeks pink with embarrassment and misery.

The three of them sat around the fire, the flames flickering and dancing, casting eerie shadows. With the soft light highlighting her beauty, Adelina was aware of Wallis's eyes straying towards her. There was a painful silence between the three of them.

Wallis drained his cup and stood up quickly. 'It's getting late. I must go.'

Instead of begging him to stay, Emily said quietly, 'Yes, Wallis.' She stood up and accompanied him to the door. Adelina remained seated in front of the fire.

When she returned, Emily stood in front of Adelina. 'I suppose you think,' she began, her voice trembling, 'that you're very clever, stealing him from me. He's the only man I've ever loved, or ever will love...' She gulped, and tears began to run down her face. At once Adelina went to her and tried to put her arm about Emily's shoulders.

'Don't touch me!' Emily cried, shaking her off.

'Emily, it's not like you think. I'm not trying to steal Wallis from you. I...' She was about to confide the real reason to Emily, but caution told her to keep quiet. Emily would be sure to tell Mrs Langley, who would see to it that Wallis did not speak to Lord Royston at all.

'The way he looks at you,' Emily was saying. 'He used to look at me like that—but not any more. I know what he's waiting for. For Lord Royston to accept you and then—then Wallis will marry you.'

Adelina gasped. Emily had half guessed Adelina's hope, but she had added far more to it than had ever entered Adelina's mind. Emily turned and ran from the room. Adelina sank back into the chair, feeling as if Emily had struck her. She closed her eyes and moaned softly. She hated being the cause of Emily's distress, but she could not give up—not yet!

The days seemed to pass so slowly, but finally Christmas came. On Christmas Eve the wassailers trudged through the village, singing their carols and stamping their feet to keep warm. At the Vicarage, even Martha Langley seemed touched by the spirit of Christmas sufficiently to unbend enough to make the revellers welcome.

Leaving the Vicarage the villagers disappeared up the lane their lusty carols echoing through the frosty night.

'Where are they going now?' Adelina asked Emily.

'To the big barn behind the Manor. The Trents always entertain the villagers at Christmas. The merrymaking goes on for days. Tonight they'll be drinking spiced ale from the wassail cup and...'

Adelina gripped Emily's arm, her eyes shining. 'Couldn't we go too, Emily?' She was eager for a little fun and laughter. The days spent at the Vicarage were depressingly dull.

'Oh, no, Adelina—not tonight. They get a little—well—merry, you know. But Wallis has promised to fetch us the day after Christmas Day. The villagers will be putting on their usual mummers' play then, and there will be plenty to eat and drink, beef and plum pudding. And dancing. No doubt you're hoping Wallis will dance with you,' Emily added bitterly. 'I'm sure you won't be disappointed.'

'Emily, please...'

But she would not listen.

The Christmas services at church seemed to bring the whole village community together—with the notable exception of Guy Trent and his love-child, Evan Smithson.

Adelina was surprised to see in the church the village girl whom she had seen with Evan in the abbey ruins, kneeling to pray and bowing her head with every semblance of piety.

Her name, Adelina had learned, was Lucy Walters.

A few pews behind the Langleys, on the opposite side of the aisle, sat Sarah Smithson and with her a man whom Adelina had not seen before. Most of the villagers were known to her now, but not this man.

Adelina nudged Emily. 'Who is the man in the check coat and cap, with Mrs Smithson?' she whispered. Emily took a hurried, furtive glance over her left shoulder.

'Henry Smithson—her husband,' she murmured.

Adelina turned to stare at him. So this was the man who had been obliged by his family to marry Sarah to hide her shame and give Guy Trent's son his name. There was bitterness written upon Henry Smithson's face and a wild anger in his eyes as his glance rested upon Lady Louisa Trent and her son Wallis, sitting in the Trent family pew.

There was a stir as the church door flew open, letting in a cold blast of wintry air. Adelina's heart skipped a beat as Lord Lynwood strode purposefully down the aisle. He stopped beside their pew and bowed to Mrs Langley and the two girls.

'Your servant, Miss Adelina,' he murmured, and almost reluctantly went to his own pew.

The service ended and Adelina found Lord Lynwood by her side. 'I shall not be thwarted this time, Adelina.' Without giving her chance to refuse, he took hold of her hand and placed it, possessively, through his arm and led her down the aisle. Adelina was aware of the gasps which ran like waves amongst the congregation.

Outside the church, Wallis, frowning heavily, faced them. 'My lord, I shall escort Miss Adelina home.'

'I think not tonight, Trent,' Lynwood said softly.

'Have you asked Mrs Langley's permission?' Wallis persisted, still glowering.

'Have you?' countered the Earl.

'It's understood that I escort the young ladies home from church, Lynwood,' Wallis drew himself up, his broad shoulders seeming massive.

'I'm sure Mama would not object—for once,' Emily put in coyly, aware that for once she could have Wallis to herself.

'Oh, very well,' Wallis said with bad grace and marched away, almost dragging Emily along with him.

Lynwood laughed aloud.

'Shh,' Adelina tugged at his arm. 'He'll hear you.'

'So?'

'Well...' then she began to smile too.

They wandered down the frosty lane and for a few moments they were alone in the dark night. He slipped his arm about her waist and drew her close to him. 'Adelina!' he whispered.

'No, my lord, no,' she said pushing him away, and yet her senses were reeling at his closeness, at his touch.

'Would you reject Wallis Trent's advances, Adelina?' Lynwood asked harshly.

'I—of course.' Then anger made her forget caution. 'There's only one thing in the world I want at this moment.'

'What's that?'

'To meet my grandfather.'

She heard Lynwood sigh, but he said nothing. How could he tell her that he had asked Lord Royston repeatedly to meet her, but the stubborn old man steadfastly refused. Lynwood took her hand once more and led her towards the front door of the Vicarage. There, beneath the light of the lamp, he turned to face her and looked down into her upturned, lovely face. He took her gently by the shoulders. 'Don't put your hopes too high, but if you like, I'll speak to him again.'

'No—Wallis said—I mean...' The words were out before she could stop them.

Lynwood frowned. 'Trent? What did he say?'

'He—he sees Lord Royston once a month. He said he would speak to him on my behalf.'

'Really?' Lynwood drawled. 'You're sure it was on your behalf and not his own?'

Abruptly he left her, his strides taking him down the path to his waiting carriage. She saw him climb into the vehicle and slam the door, making the horses shy in fright.

'Drive on!' he shouted irritably.

CHAPTER 5

During the early evening of the day after Christmas Day, the Trents' carriage drew up in front of the Vicarage. The two girls, warmly wrapped in their cloaks, were helped into the carriage by Wallis and, in only a few minutes, they arrived outside the barn at the Manor. Adelina gasped as she went in. The huge barn had been transformed. Holly and mistletoe wreaths decorated the walls and beams, and the light came from rushlights. At one end a makeshift stage had been erected and the floor was covered with rushes. As they entered the handbell ringers were playing a carol and from the onlookers—all the villagers, it seemed to Adelina—there came a soft humming.

At the opposite end of the barn to the stage a ladder led up to a hayloft and Adelina's eyes widened as she saw Evan Smithson and Lucy sitting at the edge of the open hayloft, their legs swinging over the side, watching the proceedings below them. When the bellringers had ended their carols, a motley selection of instruments was produced—drums, trumpets, pipes and fiddles—and suddenly a surprisingly tuneful, merry jig filled the barn. But amongst the rest of the villagers there was a strange reluctance to begin the dancing. They stood in small groups occasionally glancing with sullen eyes towards Wallis Trent.

They don't want us here, Adelina knew suddenly, intuitively. Wallis Trent—and those with him—were unwelcome intruders.

Wallis ignored their hostility. 'Would you care to dance, Adelina?'

'Why—I'm not sure I know how.'

Wallis bowed. 'As you wish.' He turned to Emily and led her on to the middle of the floor instead. Gradually, almost with a sullen belligerence, the villagers joined in.

Adelina watched the dancers and tapped her feet and swayed in time to the music. The rafters rang with the noise and the dancers whirled and spun, but there was no spontaneous gaiety, no laughter.

'May I have the pleasure of this dance, Miss Cole?'

Evan Smithson stood before her, his startlingly blue eyes challenging her. Adelina glanced up towards the hayloft to see Lucy pouting moodily because Evan had left her to seek out Adelina.

'I can't dance...'

'Of course you can. Come on,' Evan said and put his arm about her waist and before she could stop herself, she was amongst the dancers.

'You see, you can dance. Was that merely an excuse to avoid dancing with the likes o' me?'

Adelina laughed. 'Of course not.'

He swung her round, almost sweeping her off her feet, so that she was obliged to catch hold of him for support. He laughed aloud, his eyes glinting dangerously, warningly. 'I can be a good friend, Miss Adelina, but a dangerous enemy.'

Adelina arched her left eyebrow. 'Really?' she remarked drily, all her old instincts aroused by his threat.

'You know,' Evan said softly in her ear as the dance finally came to an end. 'You know, Miss Adelina, I like you. You're different. You're not afraid of me.'

'Afraid of you?' she laughed. 'The very idea, Mr Smithson.'

Evan gripped her wrist and his handsome face was close to her own. 'Don't tempt fate, sweet Adelina.'

There was menace in his words and in his tone. But Adelina adroitly twisted her wrist from his grasp and dropped a mocking curtsy. 'Thank you for the dance, Mr Smithson,' and moved away from him to rejoin Emily and Wallis.

When the music began again, Wallis said, 'Since you seem to have learnt the steps remarkably quickly, Miss Adelina, perhaps you will dance with *me* now?'

Inwardly, Adelina sighed. What a web of bitterness and tension and hatred existed in this village, she thought, and she seemed unwittingly to be caught in the middle of it. Wallis danced in silence, a frown upon his forehead. Adelina was aware of the eyes of the villagers upon them, and when, several times during the evening, Wallis demanded that she dance with him, she found herself increasingly embarrassed by his obvious attention to her. He danced only once with Emily, but Adelina was often in his arms.

'I shall be seeing your grandfather tomorrow, Miss Adelina.'

'Oh, Wallis, thank you. You will—let me know what he says?'

'Of course.' She felt his arm tighten about her and Adelina was acutely aware of Emily's face scarlet with misery. 'I'm sure we shall have much to discuss—after I have seen him.'

Before Adelina could reply, the music ended and Wallis led her back to Emily. As the noise died away, a voice rang out. All eyes turned to see Evan Smithson standing, none too steadily, at the top of the ladder leading to the hayloft, waving a tankard of ale in his right hand. Lucy, standing at his side, was pulling at his arm vainly trying to stop him.

'My friends,' he shouted, his words a little slurred. 'I give you a toast. To our lords and masters—our employers—our landlords—the Trents—my—my *family!* May they rot in hell!' He ended with a flamboyant gesture with his right hand, spilling beer. Suddenly he lost his footing.

Lucy tried to catch hold of him, but he slipped from her grasp. Lucy and several of the women shrieked as Evan toppled head first from the loft to the floor below. Luckily, he fell on a thick heap of straw and lay there laughing drunkenly.

Wallis clenched his fists and took a step forward towards his half-brother, his face contorted with rage. Boldly, Emily grasped his arm.

'No, Wallis, no, please. Look at your father. See how distressed he is. And the Smithsons. Please—don't make it any worse.'

'Very well, since you ask it, Emily,' Wallace muttered. 'But one of these days that fellow will go a step too far... Come, we're leaving.'

Vividly Adelina remembered the animosity which had flared between the two half-brothers when face to face.

As they threaded their way through the revellers, Adelina saw Sarah Smithson sitting in a dark corner, quietly sobbing into her hands. Nearby was Henry Smithson, an expression of hatred and resentment on his face. His hands, resting on his knees, were tightly clenched. Adelina stood on tiptoe, searching for sight of Squire Trent. He was standing on the opposite side of the barn, his shoulders slumped, his eyes steadfastly fixed upon the weeping Sarah, helpless misery etched into every line of his face.

Adelina passed the days following Christmas in a fever of anticipation, but Wallis did not come near the Vicarage. New Year came and went and still there was no word from him.

At last, towards the middle of January, Adelina could stand the waiting no longer. She must go in search of Wallis.

So one wild January day, when the clouds were black and threateningly low, Adelina slipped away from the Vicarage towards Abbeyford Manor. The wind whistled and blew her skirts. Her heart beat faster—she hated this kind of stormy, blustery weather and yet her desire to see Wallis overcame her fear.

First she went to the Manor stables. Thomas, the head stableboy, told her his master was out in the fields on Jupiter.

Minutes later she left the Manor yard, riding Stardust up the lane, through the woods and out on to the hillside. She rode towards the abbey ruins, once more in the hope of being able to see Wallis from there.

The wind blew with the force of a gale, the black clouds scudding overhead. Near the ruins she paused and looked about her. Then she saw him below her, down the hill on the far side of the stream, a dark figure on his black stallion. A group of farm labourers stood in a semi-circle around him—though keeping a respectful distance from the tossing head and stamping hooves of the temperamental horse. As she drew nearer, Adelina could see that Wallis Trent was shouting at the men, his face as dark as the storm clouds overhead. The men stared back at him—sullen obstinacy on their faces. Amongst them Adelina recognised Henry Smithson and beside him, Evan.

The young man's face was set in lines of bitterness and his eyes glittered with hatred.

'Be off with you,' curtly Wallis Trent dismissed them with a wave of his hand. 'And I'll stand no more of your insolence.'

As the men moved away, Evan's glance rested on Adelina for a moment, standing a short distance away beside her horse, waiting to speak to Wallis.

A small smile of malice quirked Evan's mouth and then he turned and followed his workmates.

Adelina thought no more of Evan. She did not even notice which direction he took, for now her whole attention was fixed upon Wallis Trent.

He dismounted and came towards her. At first she thought that the anger still upon his face lingered from the harsh words to his men. Then she realised that he was not at all pleased to see her.

'Well, Miss Cole?' The question was sharp, unfriendly. Instinctively, she knew immediately that the reason she had not seen him recently was because he had deliberately avoided meeting her.

Before she even voiced the question she must ask, she knew what his answer was going to be.

'Wallis—I—I came to look for you because you've never let me know if you've spoken to my grandfather. I was getting desperate.'

His lips curled wryly. 'That I can believe. Well—I do have some news for you, Miss Adelina Cole. Your grandfather wants naught to do with you. He does not acknowledge that he even *has* a granddaughter. Emily will remain his heiress. So, all your efforts to worm your way into his affections and have him make *you* his heiress have failed. And I shall marry Emily.'

Adelina gasped, staring up at him in disbelief. 'It—it had nothing to do with that, I just wanted to—to meet him...'

'But it would follow, wouldn't it? You had it all planned?'

'No, no,' Adelina cried, anguished. 'Is—is that what he thought?'

Wallis lifted his shoulders in a shrug. 'Who knows. He was deaf to all pleas. Lynwood tried too, so I understand, and has been doing ever since he brought you here.'

So Lord Lynwood had made repeated requests to Lord Royston for her. The thought warmed her cold heart to know that, despite his strange erratic moods, Lynwood had cared.

'You'd best make your way back to America. You're not wanted here,' Wallis Trent told her heartlessly.

Adelina turned away sick at heart, the loneliness sweeping over her. She remounted Stardust awkwardly, Wallis Trent making no move to help her, though all the while she was acutely aware of his cold eyes upon her. She wheeled her horse round, dug her heels in and set off up the slope towards the abbey ruins, scarcely knowing where she went—not caring.

Three people watched her go. Wallis Trent watched her until she reached the top of the slope and galloped towards the ruins, then he remounted his own horse and rode away in the opposite direction without a backward glance.

Later, he promised himself, he would visit the Vicarage and resume his courtship of Miss Emily Langley—Lord Royston's only heiress!

From the edge of the wood a motionless figure on horseback had observed her meeting with Wallis Trent, had watched the short exchange of conversation and their parting. Lynwood's heart twisted. Was he ever destined to watch the woman he desired meet with other men?

From the abbey ruins, still breathing hard from running, Evan Smithson crouched behind a crumbling wall and watched Adelina ride towards him.

As she drew near the ruins, it began to hail. Huge hailstones came tumbling from the laden clouds, stinging the horse and making the docile creature rear in fright.

Adelina screamed as she felt herself

falling backwards. She fell upon the wet ground and Stardust bolted. For a moment Adelina was stunned, the breath knocked from her body. She lay motionless as the wind roared in her ears and the hail beat down upon her. Her dread of storms blotted out all common sense and reason and the final rejection she had just suffered destroyed her spirit. Then she felt hands lifting her up and carrying her.

As understanding returned she realised someone had carried her into the ruins, into the cell-like room which afforded the only real shelter in the derelict abbey, and had laid her on the floor.

She looked up to see Evan Smithson standing over her.

'Well, well, well!' In the dimness of the room she could scarcely see his face. 'And what are you doing out on a wild day like this, my fine lady? Was your meeting with my dear half-brother *so* important?'

Adelina struggled to her feet, but with one strong push from his muscular arm, she found herself sprawling on the floor again.

'Not so fast, my pretty one. Now I've got you here, here you'll stay for a while.'

Fear flooded through Adelina's limbs.

She broke out in a cold sweat. There was menace in this man's tone.

All her old fighting instincts came flooding back. Fear and anger gave her strength. She watched his shadowy form and waited her moment, then with the swiftness born of terror she scrambled to her feet and made for the doorway. But Evan was too quick for her. He put out his foot and in the confined space easily tripped her so that she pitched forward, knocking her head on the rough stonework. She gave a groan of pain and lay still.

'Don't you like my company, my lady? Prefer my brother, do you? Well, we'll see how he'll like you when *I've* finished with you!'

Again Adelina made to struggle up, but now Evan grasped her arms and pulled her to her feet. His arms slipped about her waist, and his lips found her mouth in a crushing, bruising kiss—a kiss which held no affection, nor even passionate desire. It was merely a weapon of hatred and revenge. He was brutally strong. He held her easily with his left arm, her arms pinned against his chest. With his right arm Evan wrenched at the bodice of her habit, tearing away the fastenings to reveal her thin chemise. She felt herself being pushed down on to the rough floor again. In the dim light she saw his face twisted with cruel vengeance. She screamed but her cries were drowned by the gale outside and the lashing rain. And then she heard him laugh in triumph as he held her arms pinned down upon the floor above her head, while his mouth sought hers.

'No, please, Evan,' she pleaded. 'Please —let— me — go!' She writhed frantically, but he held her prisoner.

'No, no,' she screamed in terror, and he struck her across the face with the back of his hand, rendering her senseless. Then his full weight was upon her.

Suddenly it was over and he was moving away from her, leaving her exhausted, weak and bruised and filled with shame and horror and revulsion. She rolled away from him into the corner of the cell and retched, sick with humiliation and physical pain. Then she lay panting, sweating and yet shivering.

'No fine gentleman will want you now, my lady. And let me tell you, my brother thinks himself a fine gentleman.'

Adelina's whole body shook and quivered, her teeth chattered and her icy fingers trembled as she reached for her clothes and pulled on her chemise and then her habit. She found the bodice so torn that she could scarcely conceal her bosom. She was cold and yet her body was bathed in sweat, the cold, clammy sweat of panic. Against her will, pathetic sobs escaped her throat. She whimpered like a small bewildered wounded creature whom Evan had taken pleasure in hurting. He had wrought all his bitterness and hatred against the Trents upon Adelina, just because he believed Wallis Trent wanted her for himself.

She found her fear giving way to fury. She had survived the dangers of New York's waterfront, only to come all the way to England to be robbed of that which she held so dear in the place where she should have been secure—her grandfather's own village!

She saw that Evan, now fully clothed, was on the point of stepping through the doorway to leave her. Adelina scrambled to her feet. She stumbled blindly after him, rage robbing her of all sense and reason. The sky was dark and the rain falling heavily, but Evan was stepping casually over the stones which littered the ground. She began to run after him but tripped and fell. She screamed as the stones cut her hands. Sobbing wildly, she lay a moment and closed her eyes.

When she opened them she saw that Evan had stopped and was staring up at an awesome figure who was standing on top of one of the low, ruined walls, rigidly still, just waiting.

'Lynwood!' Adelina groaned. *'Oh, no!'*

Lying on the rock-strew, rough ground, the stones biting into her flesh, Adelina closed her eyes again, the shame sweeping over her once more.

Lynwood had arrived too late and was cursing himself for his delay.

From the edge of the wood he had watched her ride away from Wallis Trent towards the ruins. Then he had seen her fall from her horse, had even made the first move to reach her, but then he had seen Evan appear, lift Adelina's limp form and carry her, with apparent gentleness, into the shelter of the ruins. For the second time in the space of a few minutes, jealousy and blind rage swept through Lynwood. He wrenched his horse about and galloped like a madman through the wood with neither a thought for his own safety nor that of his horse.

He raced towards the waterfall—the scene of his very first moment of disillusionment. Years before, in his boyish innocence, Lynwood had adored and worshipped Caroline. But, in ruthless pursuit of her own happiness, she had shattered his belief in her. Out riding with him, Caroline had slipped away from Lynwood, who had searched for her with desperate anxiety, fearing she had been thrown from her horse—was lying injured or worse! Then he had come upon her unexpectedly at the waterfall—locked in the arms of her lover Thomas Cole.

And now it was all happening again—but with her daughter Adelina.

Flinging himself from his horse, Lynwood ran down the steep path, crashing through branches and undergrowth, heedless of injury, to sink down, breathless, against a rock. He was shaking, his hands sweating, his heart thudding, his breathing painful rasps. He sat with his head in his hands for some time and then, as he calmed, reason began to return and he raised his head slowly and with unseeing eyes gazed at the rushing waterfall, a more horrible picture forming in his mind's eye.

Lynwood knew something of Evan Smithson's story, knew of his hatred for the Trents—and the reason for it. Lynwood frowned, trying hard to pull a vision from his subconscious mind. As he had watched Adelina meet with Wallis Trent, he had been vaguely aware of the farmworkers moving away, but then his whole attention had been riveted upon Adelina and Wallis Trent, the jealousy surging through his being. But there was something else, something important... He must remember... He groaned from deep inside as the picture came to him. While he had watched them, with only half an awareness he had seen too a shadowy figure leave the group of workmen and set off in the opposite direction, running, running hard up the hill towards the ruins.

Lynwood sprang to his feet. Evan Smithson! He had been the running figure. He had seen Adelina meet Wallis Trent, had darted back to the ruins while they talked and had lain in wait for her. Lynwood ran up the path and threw himself at his horse, his heart bursting with sudden fear.

He had been wrong—so wrong! Adelina

would not meet Evan Smithson intentionally. Wallis Trent—yes. That was probable. But not Evan!

That outcast from the Trent family could only mean to harm her. Oh God! What have I done? He prayed as he galloped back through the wood, this time desperate to reach Adelina not to flee from her. Oh, Adelina, forgive me! Pray God I'm not too late.

But Lynwood was too late. Now, as he stood upon the broken wall and looked down upon the loathsome figure of Evan Smithson, and beyond him Adelina, bruised and hurt and weeping hysterically, he knew he was too late!

For a moment the earth reeled around him and the chasm of time opened up at his feet. The features of the man before him blurred, became those of another out of the past.

As Lynwood leapt down, it was not only Evan Smithson's, but the throat of Thomas Cole that his hands grasped and held and squeezed! There was a wild, murderous look upon Lynwood's face. Evan struggled desperately and lashed out at Lynwood's face with his fists.

Lynwood reeled backwards, releasing his hold. Evan threw himself on top of him, punching his face. Then Lynwood threw Evan over and he had the advantage. As the wind blew and the rain lashed about them, the two exchanged blow for crushing blow. Locked together they rolled over and over on the stones, their clothes becoming mud-stained and soaked. Adelina, too, watching, became wet to the skin, her hair plastered against her head. She saw Lynwood stagger to his feet and pull Evan up after him. With his left hand he held Adelina's attacker while his right hand smashed time and time into Evan's face until it was a raw, bleeding pulp. Suddenly Evan seemed to find a fresh surge of strength and he kicked Lynwood viciously in the groin. A grunt of pain escaped his lips, and he let go of Evan, bending double in agony. Evan took the advantage and turned to flee, stumbling over the rough ground. Lynwood looked up and saw his quarry escaping. Still holding his stomach, he limped after him. Adelina pulled herself to her feet and followed. She emerged from the ruins to see that Lynwood had caught Evan again, throwing himself full-length to catch him by the legs. They fell together and began to roll, legs and arms flailing, down the hillside, straight into the stream at the foot. Lynwood was the first to rise. He bent and from the rushing water pulled Evan to his feet. Again he smashed his fist into Evan's face, again and again, until at last, exhausted himself, he released his hold. Evan fell back into the stream. Without a backward glance, Lynwood staggered out of the water, grasping at tufts of slipper grass to pull himself up the bank. He stood a moment swaying slightly, panting heavily.

As he climbed painfully back up the hill towards her, she saw that blood smeared his nose and one eye was half closed and beginning to swell. Adelina huddled against the wall, while Lynwood stood before her, swaying, still panting, his arms hanging loosely by his sides.

His rage was spent, worked out upon Evan. As he looked down at her swollen, bruised face, at her torn clothes and drenched hair, all that was left was an infinite sadness, a desperate longing for what might have been and now could never be!

He bent down and touched her arm. 'Come—I'll take you home,' he said flatly.

'No, no!' She shrank against the stones.

‘I can’t—go back—there,’ she whispered, hoarsely, brokenly.

‘No—I know. I’ll take you to Lynwood Hall.’

CHAPTER 6

There was nothing else either of them *could* do. Lynwood could not desert her now, for his own remorse told him he could have prevented this tragic occurrence if it had not been for his own blind, jealous stupidity in allowing bitter memories from the past to overshadow the present and this innocent girl.

How she had been made to suffer for things past which were none of her doing! Her grandfather would not even see her, would not even acknowledge her existence because of the hurt her mother had inflicted upon him. Her relative—Martha Langley—could show her no kindness because Adelina represented a threat to the fortune so nearly within Martha’s grasp. And Lynwood himself—the bitterness of a boy forced to face reality and disillusionment had grown like a cancer to warp the mind and twist the heart of the grown man.

He could not desert her, but daily he still fought the battle to obliterate the images of Caroline and see only Adelina. Still she was to continue to suffer because of this conflict within him.

'I'll take you away,' he told her. 'To London. Perhaps there we can both forget what has happened.' But, sadly, they both knew it could not be so. Abbeyford and all that had happened would for ever be a dark shadow between them.

Dazedly, her spirit crushed, Adelina allowed Lord Lynwood to organise her life. He persuaded his mother to accompany them to London as chaperon for Adelina, and their journey, which took two days, was uneventful and uninteresting, for a steady drizzle fell the whole time.

At last, travelling through the heart of fashionable London, St James's Street, Piccadilly, they passed numerous elegant carriages, the dandies fastidiously dressed in their close-fitting trousers and high starched collars, strolling up and down.

'They're on their way to one club or another to play cards at the green baize tables—whist, faro, hazard—far into the night,' Lord Lynwood leaned forward, trying to rouse Adelina's interest. 'Fortunes can be won or lost in a single night.' But her eyes were dull and unseeing as she stared out of the carriage.

Their vehicle turned into a residential square in Mayfair and drew to a halt in front of a white terraced house. There were small cast-iron balconies outside each long window at first-floor level, and railings along the front bordering the pavement.

Lord Lynwood helped his mother from the carriage and then he led Adelina up the steps to the round-arched doorway. Inside, the comparative plainness of the exterior of the house gave way to opulence and luxury. The carpeted staircase, with white cast-iron balusters, arose from the centre of the hall and then divided into two separate flights from the first floor to the other floors.

Lord Lynwood led Adelina into the spacious drawing-room with its high arched ceiling. The decorations were in white but this austerity was offset by the vividly coloured carpet and rich, wine-coloured velvet drapes at the huge bay window. Brightly patterned silk covered the gilt sofas and chairs, and elegant spindly-legged tables and sideboards were set here and there. In one corner there was a harp, and a Chinese screen stood behind one of the sofas. Above her head hung two crystal chandeliers.

Lady Lynwood took complete charge and soon her household staff had made ready a room for her guest. It said much for her generous spirit that Lady Lynwood had demanded no explanations for the sudden arrival of Adelina—dishevelled, weeping and homeless—upon her doorstep.

Adelina was taken upstairs to a sumptuous bedroom. All the furnishings were in the Chinese style, from the carpet and wallpaper to the small table and chairs which were bamboo. Even the bed coverlet was richly patterned with oriental motifs. The whole effect was unusual and delicate. Hardly noticing her surroundings, Adelina fell into bed and closed her eyes, completely exhausted and wishing she might never wake up!

For three days Adelina kept to her room, listlessly picking at the dainty trays of food set before her, or idly lying in bed just staring at the ceiling. She neither washed her face nor brushed her hair, nor even looked into the mirror.

On the fourth day, Lady Lynwood entered the bedroom, her stick tapping determinedly on the floor. She stood at the end of the bed and regarded Adelina for several moments.

'Well, you do look a poor creature,' she said briskly, not allowing even a hint of the sympathy she felt for the girl to show in her tone. 'I don't know what happened in Abbeyford—and I don't want to,' she added swiftly. 'But, whatever it was, it doesn't warrant you moping your young life away. Now, come along, my girl. Out of that bed!'

Adelina made no move.

Smartly Lady Lynwood rapped her stick upon the end of the bed. The sudden and unexpected noise made Adelina jump and she sat up, her green eyes flashing, her auburn hair tumbling in a tousled mass about her shoulders.

'Ah—that's better,' the old lady laughed her cackling laugh. 'Some response at last!'

'Go away!' Adelina muttered. 'Just leave me alone.'

'Don't give me orders in my own house,

my girl,' Lady Lynwood snapped, and inwardly congratulated herself to see a spark of anger flash again in Adelina's green eyes.

'Come along, get up. I'm taking you shopping.' Lady Lynwood eyed the torn, stained riding-habit, the only garment Adelina now possessed. 'You have need of some new gowns, I believe,' she added wryly, and turned to leave, her cackling laughter ringing in Adelina's ears.

Within three weeks Lord Lynwood had established the unresisting Adelina in an apartment of her own—only a short distance from his own London home—and had provided her with a staff to run it, including her own personal maid. With Lady Lynwood's help, Adelina now possessed a wardrobe of fashionable gowns and accessories.

Slowly, life began to flood back into Adelina's frozen veins and the nightmare of Abbeyford receded a little—but never, ever, could it be obliterated.

A few weeks passed before Adelina began to regain her vitality and her beauty, for so deep were the emotional scars inflicted upon her. During this time Lynwood was kind and solicitous, taking her to small, select supper-parties where she did not have to meet too many people at once. But as winter gave way to spring and spring to early summer and the London Season began, Adelina was fully recovered.

Her new life in London began to intrigue and excite her.

'Well, Adelina my love,' Lynwood smiled. 'I think it is time I introduced you to the high life of Society. I shall take you to visit the Vauxhall Pleasure Gardens.'

Her excitement mounted as she dressed. From among her new gowns Adelina chose one of emerald green silk, its neckline daringly low. Diamonds clustered about her snowy throat and shone in her hair, dimmed only by the sparkle in her shining eyes. Jane, her maid, dressed Adelina's hair high upon her head with a profusion of curls framing her face.

It was masquerade night and the gardens were illuminated with hundreds of lamps. Adelina, on Lord Lynwood's arm, strolled down the long avenues lined with trees. To her eyes, all of Society seemed to be here this night. Laughter rang through the still, early summer evening air. Adelina took a deep breath, savouring the scent of the trees, marvelling at the sweet air.

'It scarcely seems credible,' she remarked to the Earl, 'that we are in the heart of the city of London.'

Lord Lynwood's eyes were upon her, admiring her beauty, trying desperately to blot out the memory of that other face so like Adelina's. She did not seem to notice, for she was still eagerly drinking in the scene around her, her lips slightly apart, her lovely face vibrantly alive. Almost against his will Lord Lynwood felt his pulses quicken and he put his hand over hers where it rested, lightly, on his arm.

At his touch she looked up at him. 'Oh, my lord, this is so wonderful. I've never—ever—seen anything like this,' she murmured, entranced. Her hand tightened on his arm in a gesture of gratitude. 'Thank you for bringing me, for making it all possible. I...' She stopped in mid-sentence and put her head slightly on one side, listening intently. 'Is that music I hear?'

'Most probably.'

'Oh, do let's find it.'

Smiling indulgently at her sudden child-like enthusiasm, Lord Lynwood led the way to the orchestra pavilion. He found that Adelina's lack of sophistication, such a contrast to her mother, helped to erase some of the memories.

They found quite a crowd mingling around the pavilion, listening to the musicians or merely engaging in conversation in select little groups.

'I say, Lynwood!' a voice greeted him out of the shadows. Adelina turned to see an elegantly dressed young man approaching.

'Eversleigh!' Lord Lynwood greeted him with genuine delight. He turned to Adelina. 'This is my good friend, Lord Peter Eversleigh.' Lynwood laid his hand upon the shoulder of the young man as he made the introductions. Lord Eversleigh bowed over Adelina's hand.

'The pleasure is all mine, ma'am.'

He was very tall, lanky rather, for he was a little to thin for his height so that he appeared to stoop slightly. He was dressed fashionably. His hair was black and curled crisply. His skin was dark and his eyes a deep azure blue. His tailed coat and trousers were of the finest material and the silk waistcoat was cut low to show a frilled shirt. He was aristocratic and elegant.

'Look, will you join me for supper?' He

turned towards Lynwood.

'Well...' Lynwood hesitated.

'Oh, come on, Lynwood. Don't keep this lovely lady all to yourself.'

For an instant a shadow crossed Lynwood's face, but resolutely he smiled and allowed his friend to lead them to one of the small supper-boxes arranged amongst the trees. Gallantly, Lord Eversleigh helped Adelina to seat herself comfortably.

'Now don't run away, Miss Cole, I beg you,' and so saying he hurried away again and was soon lost amongst the throng.

'Where has he gone?'

Lynwood sat down beside her. 'To find refreshment for us, I suspect.'

They sat in companionable silence, watching the young dandies strolling by with languid elegance and the young ladies flirting outrageously.

Lord Eversleigh returned with a manservant carrying a tray of glasses of punch and dishes of sillabub laced with wine.

'Oh, this is heavenly,' Adelina enthused as she tasted the sweet concoction.

'Indeed it is, ma'am,' Lord Eversleigh concurred, his eyes upon her face with open admiration, as if he would agree with anything and everything she said.

'Careful, my friend,' Lynwood murmured. 'You're in danger of poaching upon my preserves.'

Lord Eversleigh laughed good-naturedly.

'Oh, *there* you are, my lord!'

Adelina looked up sharply to see who had spoken. Standing close by their table was a young woman, pretty but in an overdressed, vulgar way. Her gown was revealingly low and so tight that her ample bosoms were pushed unnaturally high. Her face was heavily powdered and rouged, and her throat, arms and hair seemed covered with cheap jewellery.

'Ah, yes—Harriet. Here I am.' Lord Eversleigh rose to his feet—reluctantly, Adelina thought—and invited the girl to sit down.

'I ran into my old friend Lynwood here.'

'And decided to desert me in favour of them?' the girl snapped, her eyes smouldering. Adelina sipped her glass of punch and regarded the girl with amusement.

Colour crept slowly up Eversleigh's neck and he shuffled his feet in embarrassment. 'No—no. Of course not. I was but spending a few moments with my friends and then

I was coming back to you. I thought you were happily enjoying the music.'

'I was,' the girl countered swiftly, 'until I found you were no longer at my side.'

There was an awkward silence in which Harriet transferred her resentful gaze from Lord Eversleigh to Adelina. The two girls eyes each other speculatively.

'Well,' Harriet said petulantly, 'aren't you going to make the introductions?'

A small sigh escaped Lord Eversleigh's lips, and he said swiftly and without courtesy,

'Miss Cole—this is Harriet. Miss Adelina Cole from America.'

'America? Heavens!' The girl had the grace to look impressed. 'I thought I hadn't seen you before and I know everyone there is to know,' she added smugly.

'I guess you do,' Adelina drawled, her left eyebrow raised fractionally, her eyes never leaving Harriet's face. She recognised her at once for what she was. There had been plenty of girls like Harriet in the waterfront taverns, but despite their desperate straits, Adelina had refused to become one of them.

Obviously, Harriet was Lord Eversleigh's mistress.

Adelina was motionless, the colour suddenly creeping up her neck and over her face. She swallowed and laced her fingers together tightly in an effort to still their shaking.

That is what everyone here would think of her! That she, Adelina Cole, was Lord Lynwood's mistress. The realisation hit her with such force, left her feeling as if she stood—helpless—at the edge of a precipice, unable to take the step back to safety.

Unaware of her anguish, Lynwood watched the crowd passing back and forth before them, lost in his own brooding thoughts.

The following evening they were to attend a grand ball and Adelina dressed with supreme care. She chose an evening gown of pale blue crape over a slip of white satin. The neckline was cut square and very low. The hemline was heavily decorated with crape bows and frills.

Lord Lynwood called for her at her apartment.

'You are enchanting, ma'am,' he said and bowed deeply as she curtsied playfully to him.

Lynwood himself handed her into his

carriage and they bowled through the fashionable streets of London.

They drew up outside a grand terraced house with pillars on either side of a huge oak front door. More carriages lined the road and the night air was filled with the sound of laughter and excited chatter.

'Well,' Lord Lynwood smiled down at her as he escorted her up the steps and into the house. 'Are you ready to rock London Society?'

Adelina laughed. 'I hope so.'

As they entered, their names were announced and Adelina was aware of the heads turning, of the sudden stillness in the room, swiftly broken by the babble of speculation which swept through the vast room. The young men soon gravitated towards her and before long she was dancing every dance and never twice with the same partner—except for Lynwood, who demanded four. He watched as she danced with other men, his eyes following her swaying body, her parted lips, her shining eyes. She was easily the most beautiful girl in the room and a new face amongst the familiar ones of this particular set was bound to create excitement amongst the gentlemen and jealousy amongst the ladies.

Breathless and laughing, Adelina returned to Lord Lynwood. For the first time Abbeyford and all its unhappy memories seemed a hundred years away.

'Oh, Francis, this is wonderful. Oh look, there's Lord Eversleigh!' The use of Lynwood's Christian name sprang naturally to her lips. Now she felt his equal as his friends and contemporaries laughed and flirted with her.

But Adelina's growing confidence was like a knife in Lynwood's heart—now she was even more like her mother!

Gaily she waved her ivory fan at Lord Eversleigh across the room. Immediately he threaded his way through the people to reach her.

'Miss Cole—Lynwood. 'Tis good to see you here.' His words were intended to include them both, but his eyes rested solely upon Adelina. But her restless gaze was wandering about the room, drinking in the elegance, the atmosphere of frivolity and enjoyment. She had never known anything like it in her life. She had not known such a world even existed.

Suddenly she saw the smile fade from Lord Eversleigh's face. 'I say, Lynwood,' he said in a low, urgent tone and nodded his head towards the door.

Lynwood turned and Adelina's eyes followed the direction of his gaze. Standing at the top of the stairs, framed in the doorway, stood a beautiful woman. Adelina eyed her critically... Whoever she was, she was certainly lovely. Her skin was creamy white and her black hair shone and glinted in the light. Her low-cut gown was of transparent pink net over a deeper shade of pink.

'Who is she?' Adelina asked. She saw Lord Lynwood and his friend exchange a glance.

'That,' remarked the Earl of Lynwood drily, 'is Helene Lyon.'

'Do you know her?' Adelina asked innocently.

Lynwood coughed and Lord Eversleigh seemed to stifle his laughter.

'Slightly,' Lynwood replied, but there was sarcasm in his tone.

Helene Lyon floated elegantly down the steps, graciously acknowledging greetings on every side. She smiled and fluttered her fan, but all the while she was making her way directly across the room towards Lord Lynwood.

'Francis! How wonderful you're back in London,' she cried, stretching out her hands towards him. 'I couldn't imagine *you,* of all people, vegetating in the dreary countryside.' Helene's voice was low and seductively husky. Her eyes flirted openly with him.

'Helene.' Lynwood kissed her hand and then turned towards Adelina.

'I must introduce you to Miss Adelina Cole from America.' Now that she was close, Adelina could see that Helene Lyon's face was perfectly proportioned, with pale blue eyes, finely arched brows and full, well-shaped lips.

'How do you do?' The expression in Helene's eyes belied her friendly greeting. Her scathing glance raked Adelina from head to toe and her lip curled disdainfully. 'Are you staying in London long, Miss Cole?'

Adelina glanced at Lynwood. 'I'm not sure. I hope so, but the decision rests with Lord Lynwood.'

Adelina heard Helene's swift intake of breath and saw the anger spark within her eyes. Helene turned to face Lynwood and her eyes narrowed.

'So—that's the way it is!' She gave

a snort of contempt and turned away abruptly, her skirts swirling angrily.

'Methinks you have offended the lady,' Eversleigh murmured.

'It would appear so,' Lynwood remarked in an offhand manner. He held out his arm to Adelina, 'Come, Adelina, 'tis time you danced with *me* again.'

Watching her dance with other men had caused Lynwood to feel acute jealousy. Seeing her admired had at last made him acknowledge his own deepening passion for her.

As they joined three other couples in a quadrille, Adelina was aware, all the time, of Miss Lyon's hostile gaze following their every movement.

Adelina found herself dancing opposite a tall, thin, young dandy, whose admiration for her was plain to see.

As the dance came to an end he demanded to be introduced to her. Lynwood performed the introductions with bad grace. It was the first time Adelina had seen him openly discourteous towards someone. His lips were a thin, hard line and anger glittered in his blue eyes making them seem suddenly cold.

'Mr Thomas de Courtney—Miss Adelina Cole.'

'Madam—I am charmed. You are like a breath of spring amongst our dull company. May I pray beseech the pleasure of the next dance?'

'Of course...'

But Adelina's words were interrupted by Lynwood saying sharply, 'It's time we were leaving, Adelina.'

'Oh, no, Francis,' she spoke without thinking. 'I'm having such a wonderful time, I don't want to go yet.'

'Madam,' Lynwood said warningly, 'you will oblige me by leaving when *I* say.'

For a moment the fire of challenge was between them, their determined, wilful spirits clashing. Then colour flooded Adelina's face as she remembered that she was only here by Lynwood's kindness. She had allowed the flattery of all the young men here to turn her head for a moment. Submissively, she put her hand on his arm. 'Of course. I'm sorry, my lord.'

His anger melted at once and Lynwood caressed her cheek with the tips of his fingers. The scene did not go unnoticed by those nearby. As Lynwood led Adelina from the room it was not only Helene Lyon's eyes which followed them.

'My Lord Lynwood seems to be smitten

somewhat,' remarked one of Thomas de Courtney's friends.

'Egad, but she's a fine filly. From the New World, ain't she?' murmured de Courtney. 'I'd like to try my hand at prising her away from Lynwood.'

'Why don't you, then?'

'I might at that,' he remarked casually.

'Damned fool if you do, de Courtney. He'll call you out for sure and he's reputed to be the best swordsman this side of the Channel.'

De Courtney shrugged and his eyes followed Adelina until she left the room and disappeared from view.

'It might even be worth it if I'd had that little filly first!'

His fellow companions guffawed loudly.

In the carriage Lynwood and Adelina did not speak to each other, but each was acutely aware of the tension between them.

Lynwood, his desire, his love and all the bitter memories he'd tried so hard to crush had come crowding to the surface as he had watched Adelina dancing with other men.

He followed her into her apartment and

slammed the door behind them. Adelina gasped and whirled to face him, her eyes wide, her lips apart. At the look on his face, she backed away and put her hand out as if to fend him off. 'No, my lord, please. I...'

'Adelina!' he whispered hoarsely and reached out towards her. 'Don't be afraid. I won't—hurt you.' He grasped her shoulders and drew her into his embrace. His mouth found hers, demanding, searching, pleading for love, so that she found herself, unwilling at first, responding to his desperate need for her. His hands stroked her hair, his mouth was against her neck, his lips seeming to burn her skin. Then he picked her up and carried her towards the bedroom, kicking shut the door behind them.

He lay beside her, his arms about her. For a moment his lips were gentle, his caresses tender and worshipping, but as his passion grew, a swift change of mood overwhelmed him and he took her swiftly, using her for his own selfish gratification, punishing her for something she could not understand.

His passion spent, he still lay heavily across her, his face buried against her neck, great shuddering sobs shaking his whole being. She could feel the wetness of his tears against her skin.

Suddenly he raised himself from her and, keeping his face averted, rolled off the bed and stumbled towards the door.

As the door shut behind him, Adelina curled her lovely body into a ball as if to protect herself from further misuse.

Was there no love in this world? Were all men as cruel as this? She covered her face with her arms and sobbed and sobbed.

Eventually she fell into a deep, troubled sleep where Evan Smithson's twisted features became Lynwood's tortured face!

The following day, there was no word from Lynwood, nor on the next, but on the third day Adelina was surprised to receive a visit from Lord Eversleigh during the morning. As she bade him sit down, she noticed he seemed ill at ease.

'Er—Lynwood is—er—staying with me.'

Adelina raised her left eyebrow fractionally. 'Really?'

'He—er—asked me to come and—well—see if you were still here.'

The silence grew between them and then Lord Eversleigh's eyes met Adelina's steady gaze.

'Yes,' she said quietly. 'I am still here.'

'And—and are you going to stay?'

Slowly she inclined her head. 'Yes.'

Relief flooded through his face. 'Lynwood will be glad. He's very fond of you, you know, Miss Cole.'

'Did he tell you to say that?'

'No—no—but I know he is. I can tell.' Eversleigh stood up. 'He'll be back this evening, then.'

'Tell him...' Adelina paused.

'Yes?' Eversleigh queried eagerly.

'Tell him—I look forward to seeing him.'

Eversleigh smiled. 'I will.'

After Lord Eversleigh had left, Adelina decided she would not remain closeted within her rooms any longer. She would go driving in Hyde Park that afternoon.

So, at five o'clock, the fashionable time when all the Society people appeared to drive or ride in the Park, she sent word that she required Lord Lynwood's carriage. Her arrival there caused a stir amongst those who went there regularly. Adelina recognised one or two faces from her attendance at the ball and, before many minutes had passed, she found that several of the young men on horseback were keeping pace with her carriage. One seemed determined to get close to her.

'Why, it's Mr de Courtney, is it not?'

'It is, ma'am, and I am mighty flattered that you should have remembered my name. I, of course, could not forget yours if I had tried. Indeed, Miss Cole, my *dear* Miss Cole, you have been scarcely out of my thoughts since I laid eyes on you the other evening.'

'Really, Mr de Courtney?' Adelina knew his words to be outrageous flattery. 'Aren't you going to introduce me to some of your companions?' she nodded towards the other riders beside her carriage.

'What? And have them usurp my place beside you, Miss Cole? Indeed I am not!'

Her carriage had slowed to a snail's pace so that she might carry on a conversation with Thomas de Courtney. Several other carriages rattled past.

'Why, there's Miss Lyon!' Adelina waved her gloved hand in greeting, but Helene Lyon appeared not to have noticed, for, although she seemed to be looking in Adelina's direction, her eyes wore a steely, glazed expression.

'Why,' Adelina cried with a spurt of

anger. 'She cut me!'

Thomas de Courtney guffawed loudly. 'Are you surprised?'

Adelina's eyes widened as she looked at him. 'I don't understand you.'

'You can hardly expect her to show friendliness towards the lady who has taken her place, can you?'

Adelina looked puzzled and shook her head slightly. Brutally, Thomas de Courtney took great pleasure in informing her, 'Helene Lyon was Lynwood's mistress. That is until you arrived on the scene.'

'What makes you think I am his mistress?' Adelina snapped defiantly.

'Oh, come now, Miss Cole,' Mr de Courtney waved his hand towards the numerous ladies in their carriages, most of whom seemed to be engaged in conversation with some gentleman. 'There isn't one of these lovely ladies here who hasn't a string of lovers to her name. It's the occupational pastime of the idle rich, my dear.'

Adelina opened her parasol. 'Well, Mr de Courtney. I am not a Britisher—so pray don't judge *me* by your own standards!'

'Brave words, Miss Cole, but I wonder just how long you'll be able to live up to such a high moral code if you plan to become part of our decadent Society?'

Adelina declined to answer. 'Drive on,' she instructed her coachman sharply. 'Goodbye, Mr de Courtney.'

'Goodday, Miss Cole. We shall meet again.'

Adelina was in a fine temper when she arrived home, partly because she had found Thomas de Courtney's arrogance disturbing but more so because he, and most likely everyone else, had recognised her for just what she had become—the mistress of Lord Francis Lynwood.

Jane was waiting for her. 'His lordship has sent word he is taking you to dine tonight, madam, and afterwards to the Opera.'

'The Opera!'

Adelina's ill-humour was dispelled in an instant. 'How wonderful! I've heard such a lot about it, but I've never been. Oh, Jane, what shall I wear? How shall I dress my hair?'

When Lynwood greeted her that evening it was as if the unhappy incident between them had never occurred. He bowed to her. 'You look exquisite, my love. I shall be the envy of all the young men present.'

Taking her cue from him, Adelina smiled. 'And I shall be the envy of all the fine ladies with the handsome Lord Lynwood as my—escort.' She hesitated fractionally over the last word, for she had been about to say 'lover', but had thought better of it. She did not want to quarrel with Francis, though she longed to challenge him about Helene Lyon.

'I hope you don't mind,' Lynwood told her as they sat side by side in the carriage. 'I have invited Eversleigh and his wife to dine with us.'

So, Eversleigh was married, yet kept a mistress too!

'His wife?' Adelina asked with sarcasm. 'Not—Harriet?'

In the darkness of the carriage, she heard Lynwood laugh wryly. 'No—not on this occasion, though no doubt Eversleigh would have preferred her.'

Adelina was puzzled by the remark until she saw Lady Madeleine Eversleigh for herself. The poor woman was cursed with a face which could only be described as plain—and then if one were being very kind. She had a long, oblong-shaped face, with a hooked nose and eyes set too close together and a row of huge teeth which protruded alarmingly. Her teeth seemed to fill her whole mouth! Despite the disadvantage of her looks, Lady Eversleigh seemed a kindly creature whose desire to be friendly and to please was almost pathetic. It was also obvious to Adelina's shrewd eye that the poor woman was deeply in love with her handsome husband and equally obvious that he did not return her devotion.

The dinner was sumptuous. Everything was served on silver plates and dishes. Hot soups and salmon, a saddle of mutton and a selection of cold meat dishes too. Iced champagne was served and then bowls of peaches, grapes, pineapples and all manner of fruit were placed within easy reach.

Afterwards they went to the Opera House. During the interval after the First Act, Adelina looked about her again. She was intrigued by the finery of the ladies and the dandies. She leant forward to look down into the pit, fascinated to see the fops strolling about showing off the fine cut of their new clothes, elegantly taking snuff from jewelled snuff-boxes and chattering noisily, even throughout the performance.

Adelina's eyes took in every detail of the

rich and ornate surroundings, scanning the gallery and the boxes, admiring all the fine gowns of the ladies. This was the world to which her mother had belonged—and now Adelina was part of it too.

As they drove home in the darkness of the carriage, she was surprised to feel Francis search for her hand and clasp it, holding it tenderly. It was as if he was trying to communicate an apology to her. She was touched by his concern, by his desire to rectify matters between them. She blinked back the tears, smiled tremulously and squeezed his hand in return.

That night when Lynwood stayed with her once more, Adelina learnt that there could indeed be a different kind of lovemaking to the brutal ways she had hitherto experienced. Lynwood was gentle, seeming to give rather than to take, so that she found her fears falling away and her natural sensuality responding to his caresses.

But even at the height of their passion she was acutely aware that there was a bitterness in Lynwood's heart.

So many shadows lay between them.

Thomas de Courtney had been quite

correct when he said they would meet again, for some weeks later Lynwood took her to a private party where card-playing and gambling were to take place. The weeks since her arrival in London had been filled with balls, suppers, routs and sightseeing, but this was the first party she had attended where the main interest was to be gambling.

The moment she entered the room Adelina was dismayed to see Mr de Courtney and Helene Lyon deep in conversation on the far side of the room. Adelina put her hand on Lynwood's arm possessively. He smiled down at her and, out of the corner of her eye, she saw Miss Lyon's face grow dark with anger. Adelina smiled and nodded to those who greeted her. Her confidence had grown and she moved with ease now in Lord Lynwood's world. He led her about the room, introducing her to those she had not met before and greeting those she already knew. Eventually they stood in front of Mr de Courtney and Miss Lyon.

'So, we meet again, Miss Cole,' Mr de Courtney gave an elegant but exaggerated bow.

'So it seems,' Adelina replied tartly, all

the while watching Miss Lyon's face as she smiled and fluttered her eyelashes at Lord Lynwood.

'Why, Francis,' Helene Lyon purred in her husky voice. 'It seems an age since I saw you. Now, let me see, whenever was it—ah, I remember. When you were staying with Lord Eversleigh for a night or two.' Her glance slanted meaningly towards Adelina.

Adelina stiffened and almost a gasp of surprise escaped her lips, but with supreme control she managed to keep her features composed, for she knew the woman was merely trying to goad her. So, she thought, seething inwardly, Francis had found comfort in Miss Lyon's arms, had he? And, not only that, the whole of Society must know that he and she had quarrelled and that he had found refuge with Eversleigh—and with Helene Lyon!

Once out of earshot of Miss Lyon and away from her scheming eyes, Adelina snatched her hand away from Lynwood's arm. She heard him sigh softly.

'Adelina, Eversleigh and I went to a private card party and Helene—Miss Lyon—happened to be there.'

Adelina was surprised and shaken to

find how the thought of Helene Lyon in Lynwood's arms hurt her desperately. But she would not let him know that. Proudly she said, 'I'm sure it's of no consequence where you were—or whom you were with,' she added pointedly. Then she turned swiftly to face him. 'But pray credit me with a little intelligence in such matters, Francis. I know of your liaison with—*her!*'

'I'll not deny it, my love. But that was before I even met you. I have not visited her since then.' He seemed almost surprised himself at the fact.

Adelina searched his face but from his expression he gave every appearance of telling the truth.

There was a stir of excitement in the room as the gaming-tables were set up and the serious business of the evening began.

As the night wore on, one or two of the men, befuddled by drink, began to lose money consistently and heavily. To Adelina the huge sums of money the dandies wagered were ridiculously large. Despite their obvious wealth she could not imagine how their finances could stand such depletion. She was not enjoying the evening, for the gambling reminded her of her father and the unhappiness it had caused them both.

Lynwood and Eversleigh were playing at a table with Thomas de Courtney and another young dandy, Geoffrey Dalton, a fair-haired, pale-skinned and somewhat effeminate man. Mr de Courtney had become decidedly tipsy from the numerous glasses of wine he had consumed. He seemed to lose all sense of caution, betting wildly on his cards when experience should have told him he had no chance of winning with such a hand. Adelina stood quietly behind Lynwood's chair, watching. She knew that both he and Eversleigh were finding the game an embarrassment now rather than a pleasure.

'Well, I think I'll call it a day,' Eversleigh said, attempting to break up the game.

'What?' De Courtney gripped Eversleigh's arm drunkenly. 'Tha's right, try to walk away with all the winnings without giving a fellow time to redeem himself. Call yourself a gen—,' he hiccupped loudly, 'gentleman?'

'You're drunk, de Courtney,' Lynwood said bluntly. 'You'd do better to leave the table now before you lose even more of your inheritance than you've lost already.'

'No damn business of yours, Lynwood, if I lose the lot!' He banged his fist down on the table, making the cards jump and the money rattle.

Lynwood shrugged. 'Have it your own way, then.'

'Tell you what, Lynwood,' de Courtney leant towards him, but his glance leered up at Adelina standing behind Lord Lynwood's chair. 'I'll play you one hand for the greatest prize of all! My entire inheritance against your whore!'

There was a moment's stunned silence about the table and then startled gasps and shocked murmurings.

Lynwood leapt to his feet, overturning the table, scattering cards and money in all directions and even knocking poor Lord Eversleigh on to the floor.

Lynwood's face was a picture of terrifying and revengeful rage. He grasped de Courtney by the lapels of his jacket and hauled him to his feet. Then his strong fingers gripped de Courtney's throat, choking him so that his face grew purple and his eyes bulged. Eversleigh pulled at Lynwood's arm.

'Lynwood—for God's sake. You'll throttle him.'

Other hands began to reach forward to separate Lynwood's murderous grasp from de Courtney's neck.

Adelina tried to swallow the fear rising in her throat. There was maniacal revenge in Lynwood's eyes. It was not only de Courtney beneath those fingers but Evan Smithson and Thomas Cole too! Time after time, it seemed to Lynwood, other men came between him and the girl he loved. Now here was a conceited dandy calling Adelina the most insulting name he could think of, and yet wanting her for himself.

'Lynwood! *Lynwood!'* The fear in Eversleigh's voice penetrated Lynwood's mind and slowly he relaxed his hold.

De Courtney slipped to the floor—unconscious. Lynwood stood over him, swaying slightly, breathing hard, his arms hanging loosely at his sides. Several ladies screamed and decided they should faint, but since all attention seemed to be on the prostrate de Courtney, they thought better of it and contented themselves with fanning their hot faces vigorously.

Geoffrey Dalton, de Courtney's foppish young friend, gasped, 'You've killed him—you've killed him.'

'Nonsense,' Eversleigh declared stoutly, but Adelina could see the worry in his eyes. 'Lynwood, come, man, sit down.' He turned his dazed friend around and led him to a couch. The others closed around de Courtney still lying on the floor.

Adelina ran to Lynwood, sat beside him and slipped her hand into his. His fingers gripped hers, clinging to her and together they watched until the circle around de Courtney parted and they saw him sitting up on the floor, holding his throat and coughing.

'Oh, Francis—he's alive. He's—he's all right.'

Geoffrey Dalton stood before Lynwood and Eversleigh rose and faced him.

'De Courtney will demand satisfaction,' he sneered. 'When he's sufficiently recovered from your cowardly attack to meet you in a fair duel!'

Lynwood stood up, in complete control of his emotions now, his coolness belying the blind rage of only minutes ago.

'Any time, Dalton!'

And with that he strode from the room. Adelina and Eversleigh hurrying after him. She plucked at Lynwood's arm.

'Francis—I don't want you to fight on

my account. Please don't. Lord Eversleigh,' she appealed to their friend. 'Please help him.'

There was a moment's silence before Eversleigh said quietly. 'We can't back out now, Miss Cole, it would seem like cowardice to withdraw from such a challenge.'

'But—but what is going to happen?'

Neither answered her, but she saw them glance at each other, their faces grim and serious.

CHAPTER 7

The duel—when all the arrangements had been made between the contestants' seconds, Lord Eversleigh acting for Lynwood and Geoffrey Dalton for de Courtney—was scheduled to take place four days after the challenge had been made, on the Heath at dawn.

In the long hours of darkness Adelina felt physically sick with fear at the thought of what might happen to Lynwood. As she tossed and turned, unable to sleep, slowly the realisation came to her. She loved him! Adelina had fallen in love with Lord Lynwood, so deeply that the thought of losing him, even the thought of him being wounded, filled her with a kind of panic she had never before experienced. Even the death of her father, sudden and shocking though it had been, had not caused her such nightmarish anguish. Now she knew why she had stayed with him, had become his mistress. Even then, without knowing it, she must have loved him.

Early on the morning of the duel, when it was still dark, she slipped from her warm bed and, shivering, for the maid had not yet lit a fire in her bedroom so early was the hour, she began to dress herself. Lynwood had forbade her to attend the scene of the duel, but Adelina could not keep away. She was so afraid that Francis would be hurt, perhaps even killed, that she could not sit at home, waiting for the dreadful news. She just had to be there. She pulled the hood of her black velvet cloak well down over her face and left her apartment. She hurried along the deserted streets until she came to Lynwood's house. Slipping down the stairs to the servant's entrance, she rapped on the kitchen door.

It must be five o'clock already and she knew Francis would have left. The servants were already about their early morning tasks, so she was soon able to despatch a young footman to have Lynwood's phaeton brought immediately to the front door. Adelina paced the pavement in a ferment of anxiety. She planned to drive herself and yet she was not quite sure how she should get to the Heath. As the young footman assisted her into the phaeton, she grabbed him by the arm.

'You'll have to come with me to show me the way. If I get lost, I'll never find my way through this maze of streets, and I'll miss the whole thing.'

'But, madam,' stammered the unfortunate young man, 'my duties—I have work to do—I can't come...'

'You can and you will. I'll explain later,' she replied hastily, almost pulling him into the phaeton.

Eventually they arrived on the Heath just as the first pale fingers of dawn stretched their way over the grass. The Heath, partially shrouded in morning mist, appeared to be deserted.

'Are you sure this is the right place?' Adelina asked worriedly.

'Yes, ma'am. This is where they normally hold the duels.'

Adelina shuddered. 'You make it sound like a regular occurrence?'

The young footman shrugged. 'It seems to be, madam, amongst the dandies who have naught better to do.'

Adelina cast him a severe, disapproving glance and the man apologised hastily. 'I beg your pardon, ma'am.'

She nodded. 'I should think so, too. It's not for you to judge your master.' Then she added, 'Look, we're right out in the open here. Isn't there somewhere we can conceal ourselves? I don't want to be seen if I can avoid it.'

The footman pointed. 'Over there, there's a clump of bushes. They'll just about hide the phaeton.'

'Fine.' Adelina manoeuvred the horses until the vehicle was standing behind the bushes, hidden, she hoped, from view from the duelling place. She alighted and found a place amongst the bushes where she was concealed from view and yet she had a good view of the scene.

Scarcely had she settled herself before she saw a carriage and pair loom out of the mist and come to a halt some distance away. Though she strained her eyes to see through the mist, she could only see two figures alight from the vehicle and stand talking together. A second, smaller carriage appeared, but only one person got down, and he too, remained near his vehicle and made no move to speak to the other two.

The footman, who had come to crouch amongst the bushes beside her, whispered, 'That fellow on his own, that'll be the surgeon.'

'Surgeon!' Adelina squeaked and then clapped her hand to her mouth, fearful that her voice would be heard and she would be discovered and sent away. She lowered her voice to an urgent whisper. 'What do you mean—surgeon? Do you mean someone *always* gets hurt?'

'Or killed,' the young footman replied nonchalantly.

Adelina bit her lip hard. At that moment yet another carriage drew up not many paces from her hiding-place. She drew breath sharply as she recognised the vehicle and saw, a moment later, Lynwood and Lord Eversleigh step from its interior. They were so near she could hear their conversation plainly.

'This is a fool's errand you're on,

Lynwood,' Eversleigh said. 'He's reputedly an expert with an épée.'

Lynwood remained grimly silent.

The minutes ticked by and Adelina began to wish they would get on with the wretched duel if there was to be one. She was becoming very cramped, squatting in this undignified position in the bushes. The dank morning was seeping through her cloak and making her shiver and the mist had dampened her hair, plastering tiny curls around her face.

At that moment the surgeon moved out to the centre of the field and the protagonists' two seconds stepped forward, to converse with him.

'He's acting as referee,' whispered the footman in Adelina's ear. 'He's asking them to settle the matter without bloodshed. It's only a formality of course, no one ever does when it's got to this stage.'

In confirmation of his words, she saw Lord Eversleigh and Mr Dalton shake their heads.

Moments later the two duellists stepped forward and faced each other. The thin blades glittered and shivered as, on guard, they circled each other warily. De Courtney lunged but Lynwood parried by dropping the point of his épée down sharply and holding off his opponent's weapon. Again on guard they circled. Each lunged and parried alternately, and this gamesmanship seemed to Adelina to go on interminably.

'I think they're enjoying it!' she muttered, impatiently.

She shivered and blew on to her frozen fingers in an effort to warm them.

Suddenly Adelina saw Francis lunge and the point of his rapier disappeared into de Courtney's chest. The latter gave a cry of pain which rent the still morning and startled the onlookers, even though they were half expecting it. Thomas de Courtney sank to the ground, Lynwood's rapier still embedded in his body. The surgeon rushed forward and immediately took hold of Lynwood's weapon. Gently he eased the blade from de Courtney's chest and threw it to one side. Then he dropped to his knees beside the still form. Eversleigh and Geoffrey Dalton ran forward, one to stand at Lynwood's side while Dalton fell to his knees beside his friend.

From her position, Adelina could not hear what was said, merely a low murmuring of voices.

'We should go now, madam,' whispered the footman. ' 'Tis over and his lordship is unharmed.'

'No—they'll hear us—I don't want Lord Lynwood to know I was even here—you understand?' She pressed his arm warningly.

'Of course, madam.'

They remained hidden until Lynwood and Eversleigh had crossed the grass towards their carriage. Their faces were grim and neither of them spoke to each other. They climbed into the vehicle, which, seconds later, moved away. The prostrate form of Thomas de Courtney had not moved, and both the surgeon and Mr Dalton were still bending over him.

'Oh God,' Adelina whispered. 'I think he really has killed him this time.' She stood up, easing her aching limbs, and pulled her cloak closer around her. Her teeth were chattering with cold. 'Come on, let's get away from here before we're discovered!'

She had not expected Lynwood would visit her apartment immediately, but she had only managed to take off her damp cloak and rough dry her long hair with a towel when she heard the sound of a carriage in the street below, his footsteps pounding up the stairs and the door of her apartment flung wide open.

Lynwood strode into her bedroom and then stopped in surprise. 'Awake already, my love?' Though his tone was bantering, Adelina could detect the tension beneath the surface. She seated herself before the mirror and began to brush her long, shining hair. They each seemed to be waiting for the other to speak.

'So,' Adelina remarked with apparent indifference, even though her heart was thudding and her hands were wet with sweat, 'you managed not to get yourself killed this morning.'

Lynwood came to stand behind her, watching her through the mirror. 'You don't seem very concerned, madam?' The cynical smile twisted his mouth.

'Well—you're here, aren't you?' she raised an eyebrow.

'Don't you want to know what happened to de Courtney?'

'Did you—kill him?'

'To be honest—I don't know. He was still breathing when I left the field, but the injury was—severe. In any case,' Lynwood bent down, putting his face close to hers, though they still looked at each other through the looking-glass, 'it would be better if I were away from town until the scandal has died down a little. We shall be leaving tonight for Lynwood Hall. My mother, too, since, this time, you will have to stay at the Hall.'

Adelina's mouth fell open and her eyes widened with horror at his statement. 'Oh, no, Francis, I can't go back there. It's too near Abbeyford. Don't ask me to!'

'Well,' Lynwood muttered, 'we have no choice!'

The last thing in the world Adelina wanted was to return to the vicinity of Abbeyford and all its bitter memories. She cringed at the thought and closed her eyes and groaned.

'You promise we'll come back to London once the scandal of the duel is all over?' she begged him.

'Yes, yes,' was his impatient reply, anxious to put distance between himself and his victim's family and friends, who, he knew, would shortly be howling for his blood in revenge for the injury he had inflicted upon de Courtney.

Lynwood Hall was every bit as beautiful as Adelina remembered it. But now, having tasted the exhilarating, busy life of Society London, she soon found her life at Lynwood Hall, though comfortable, was dull and tedious.

Lynwood was withdrawn and moody. He went out most days on his own, shooting on his estate, leaving Adelina with only Lady Lynwood, his mother, for company.

'So, Miss Cole, I suppose you think you have progressed in the world since you were last here?' Lady Lynwood gave a short cackle of laughter, her bright eyes sharp and perceptive. Adelina raised her left eyebrow. She enjoyed the verbal sparring with Lady Lynwood, for beneath the surface there was a good deal of respect for each other's strength of character.

'That's a matter of opinion. Mrs Langley would not agree with you.' Nor Adelina thought sadly to herself, would her grandfather.

Lady Lynwood's piercing eyes scanned Adelina's face. 'Have you any regrets about becoming a courtesan, miss?'

Adelina winced, startled by Lady Lynwood's bluntness. 'I'm not exactly that,' she bridled, 'though I'll not deny being your son's mistress.'

'Is he—kind to you?' The sharp, all-knowing eyes were boring into her very soul. Adelina felt the colour creeping up her neck.

'Yes,' she said, determinedly shutting her mind to the times when Lynwood's dark, brooding moods overshadowed both their lives. 'Yes—of course he is!'

Lady Lynwood eyed her, shrewdly disbelieving. 'Poor Francis,' she murmured. 'I wonder if he can ever hope to find real happiness? He was badly hurt by—a woman a long time ago.'

'Who?'

'Oh, I can't tell you that,' Lady Lynwood said. 'He was only a boy. A boy's first love. It can be very painful, you know.' The old eyes, still bright and vital, regarded Adelina.

'I—guess so,' the young girl said. Then with sudden understanding, 'And you mean it—it still hurts him now?'

Lady Lynwood nodded. 'I mean that it has affected his whole attitude towards women and—love.'

'I—see,' Adelina murmured. 'Perhaps I can help him to forget her.'

'I doubt it. I think it most likely you are a constant reminder.'

But Adelina, deep in her own thoughts of Lynwood, of her love for him, remembering his many kindnesses to her, the many times when his lovemaking had been tender and joyful, failed to question the full meaning behind Lady Lynwood's words.

Lord Lynwood arranged a Meet of the local Amberly and Abbeyford Hunt as a little diversion for Adelina.

'I am Joint Master with Wallis Trent,' he told Adelina, 'but he declined to join us this time.'

She felt Lynwood's eyes upon her, watching her face for any sign of emotion at the mention of Wallis Trent's name. Still the memory of her meeting Wallis Trent on the hillside above Abbeyford haunted him, fusing in his mind with that other meeting of so long ago.

The Hunt met at Lynwood Hall. Adelina was the only woman to ride with them, though there were several ladies in their carriages from neighbouring estates who came to watch the Hunt, following as best they could along the narrow lanes and rough cart-tracks.

The morning was bright and cold and Adelina was ready early, determined to enjoy the new experience despite Lynwood's black mood. She wore a new emerald green riding-habit which she knew suited her to perfection, contrasting as it did with her rich auburn hair and making her eyes a brighter green than ever. The long skirt billowed out as she rode, the tight-fitting jacket accentuating her tiny waist.

Lynwood looked extremely handsome in his Master's coat. He greeted Adelina with his half-mocking smile, yet she could see the desire leap in his eyes. 'That habit becomes you, my love.'

'Thank you, kind sir,' she laughed and was surprised to find how much his casual compliment meant to her.

The horses and hounds moved off and, gathering speed, they pounded across the countryside. Suddenly a fox broke covert, and the hounds, barking shrilly, were in pursuit, the huntsmen hotfoot after them. Adelina felt the thrill of the chase. The fox was well ahead, running across Lord Lynwood's estate and on to the Trents' lands, through the woodland across the brow of the hill and past the abbey ruins and on yet farther. Then the hounds were gaining ground as the poor, harried creature began to tire.

The huntsmen's blood-thirsty cries echoed across the valley. Then the hounds were upon the fox, brutally ravaging, their sharp teeth tearing the animal limb from limb. Adelina reined in and sat upon her horse watching in horrified silence. She had not imagined the kill would be so nauseating.

Beside her she heard one of Lynwood's neighbouring landowners remark languidly, 'Lynwood—don't forget we have a new member of the Hunt with us. I think she should be bloodied.'

Cries of assent arose from the other men.

Lynwood laughed. 'Not satisfied with the day's sport, gentlemen?' he said with sarcasm. 'Very well.'

He dismounted and with another huntsman went amongst the hounds to return a few moments later with the decapitated head of the fox in his hand, the red blood dripping through his fingers.

He stood beside Adelina's horse. For a moment Lynwood hesitated. He was remembering that other time, the occasion of his own initiation. Then Caroline had been watching, smiling with congratulation.

'You'll have to dismount, my dear,' he

said now to Adelina.

'What are you going to do?'

'You'll see.'

Reluctantly, Adelina dismounted and stood before him. Holding her arm firmly with his free hand so that she could not draw back, Lynwood raised his hand and pressed the raw and bleeding head upon Adelina's face, moving it across her forehead and once down each cheek, accompanied by cheers of encouragement from the watchers.

Adelina screamed!

In that moment she saw Lord Lynwood's face change from amusement to anger. He put his face close to hers. 'How dare you make a sound? It's a disgrace to be cowardly at this ceremony. And you have humiliated me by being so!'

Swiftly he turned his back upon her and strode back to his horse. The onlookers were quiet now, watching her with silent disapproval. Without a backward glance at her, Lynwood rode away and, one by one, the huntsmen followed, until she was left alone.

Adelina rubbed at the blood, drying now, on her face and spattered down the bodice of her lovely riding-habit.

'What a barbaric custom,' she exploded angrily, but there was no one to hear her. 'And to think the British have the audacity to think us Yankees wild and uncivilised. Oh!' she cried and stamped her foot in rage. She remounted and spurred her horse to a gallop back towards Lynwood Hall where, she went straight away to her room to change and clean the blood from her face.

Jane's cry of indignation was fuel to Adelina's own anger and disgust. 'Oh, madam, your face and your beautiful habit. It's a disgrace and no mistake!'

Gently, Adelina sponged the blood from her face, wincing slightly as she did so. Once clean again she stared at herself in the mirror. There, for all to see, was the reason for her screams. Across her forehead and down each cheek were two scratch marks, one quite deep so that even now it oozed blood—her own. The other, fainter scratches, merely marking the surface of the skin.

'Just wait till his lordship sees *that!*' Adelina thought, and said aloud, 'Jane, go and find out what is happening downstairs.'

After a few moments her maid arrived

back a little breathless. 'His lordship is in the library, madam, with all his guests—the gentlemen, that is. The ladies are in the drawing-room.'

Adelina nodded, her eyes gleaming with satisfaction. Regally, she descended the stairs and went towards the library. A footman opened the door for her and stood, just inside the doorway, watching the assembled company.

One of Lynwood's guests was the first to notice her standing there. His mouth dropped open at the sight of her lovely face marked by the ugly scratches. He nudged Lynwood, who turned and then, gradually, every gentleman in the room had seen her and everyone fell silent.

Adelina saw the last traces of anger, which still lingered in Lynwood's expression, disappear at the sight of her.

She saw his lips form her name in a soft whisper, saw the mute apology in his eyes. He made a step towards her, but Adelina, satisfied to have proved her point not only to Lynwood but to all his aristocratic friends as well, turned on her heel and walked sedately through the hall and into the drawing-room.

Later, when all his guests had departed,

Lynwood sought her out.

'Adelina—my love,' his voice was hoarse. 'I apologise most humbly. I had no idea. It must have been a sharp piece of bone sticking out.'

He held out his arms to her and, with a little sob, Adelina turned to him and was enfolded in his embrace. He held her close, murmuring endearments, whilst she wound her arms about him and hugged him.

That night their lovemaking was the joyous, tender union of two people who loved each other—yet still neither could speak aloud the very words the other so longed to hear.

Still the shadows were between them!

The weeks and months passed and still no word came that they could return to London. Adelina, when Lynwood left her alone, took long, solitary rides on horseback to try to alleviate the boredom.

So far, she had kept away from Abbeyford, but one afternoon she found herself, almost against her will, taking the road through Amberly and towards Abbeyford. She felt an overwhelming desire to hear news of her grandfather. There had never been a day pass—even during the time she had spent in London—when she had not thought of him. A shadowy figure built in her imagination from the faded miniature in her locket. If only she could meet him—just once—so that she could carry a true likeness of him in her mind.

There was a need to see him, a need to feel close, for over the past two weeks there had been a secret fear in her mind, a fear she had not even confided to Lord Lynwood. But if it were to be true—then she had more need than ever of her family.

Though it was still March and the air sharp, the sun was bright.

As she passed through the village of Amberly, a crowd of ragamuffin, barefoot children gaped at the fine lady on horseback. Then one boy, older than the rest, recognised her.

'Why, it's 'er as went an' ran off to London wi' Lord Lynwood. Ha-ha—you know what *she* is? She's 'is whore!'

Suddenly something hit her horse's flanks, making the animal rear and snort and then bolt, with the sound of the children's laughter ringing in her ears. Adelina, though startled, managed to keep her seat and soon brought the animal under control once more. The boy had thrown a stone at her! Adelina was outraged. She turned her horse round to ride back and give the boy a box on the ears. As she did so she saw that now the crowd of children were ranged across the road and all were armed with missiles. A shower of stones and sticks came towards her and, though she was too far away to be in danger of being hit this time, the children's actions and their cries of derision unsettled her horse again. Adelina noticed that several of the women had now appeared in the doorways of their cottages, but far from chastising their children, they appeared to be encouraging them.

Adelina turned her horse about again and spurred him into a gallop. When at last she slowed to a trot again, she herself was breathless, her cheeks aflame, her eyes bright and sparkling with anger, her auburn hair flowing loose and free.

And this was how Wallis Trent saw her again.

He was on his way, riding his black stallion, Jupiter, to Amberly village when, cresting the hill, he saw Adelina riding towards him. He reined in and sat upon his horse, watching her. Still thinking of the insults of the village children, Adelina did not see him until she was upon him. She pulled on the reins and her horse stopped.

Wallis's face was expressionless.

'Mr Trent,' Adelina greeted him cautiously.

At last he spoke. 'So Miss Cole, you have dared to return. I doubt you'll find much of a welcome in this vicinity.'

'I did not expect one, Mr Trent,' she replied tersely. 'I merely wish to—to enquire after my grandfather. Is he well?'

Wallis Trent smiled, a small quirk on his lips, but there was no pleasantness. 'Your determination surprises me, Miss Cole. Are you *still* harbouring hopes of reconciliation?' He laughed sarcastically. 'You're wasting your time.'

'Is he well?' Adelina persisted, determined to have him answer her.

'Yes, he's well.' Wallis Trent leaned forward, his eyes hard and cold, boring into her. 'Happily anticipating the arrival of my son. He's already made a generous settlement upon the child—even before its birth!'

Adelina gasped. So Wallis Trent and Emily were married and she was to have a child. A child who would eventually inherit Lord Royston's entire estate.

Adelina did not care about the inheritance, but the news did make her feel even more excluded from the family to which she rightfully belonged. Lord Royston's affection was to be lavished upon Emily's child—instead of upon his own granddaughter. She swallowed the lump in her throat and raised her head in proud defiance. She would not let Wallis Trent see how the news upset her, but she could not bring herself to speak the words of congratulation.

'So your inheritance slips a little further out of reach, my dear.'

'I care not for my inheritance—I've told you that!'

But how could she expect an avaricious man like Wallis Trent to understand her longing to be loved, her need to belong?

'Wallis,' Adelina asked suddenly. 'What—what happened to Evan?'

Wallis shrugged. 'He disappeared from the village the same night as you. For a time it was thought that you and he...' His eyes glinted. 'Then we heard you were with Lynwood.' His lips curled disdainfully.

Embarrassment coloured her face at the

innuendo in his tone. And then fear crept into her heart. That night—had Lynwood killed Evan? She swallowed, torn between the desire to know the truth and the need to protect Lynwood. He was in enough trouble already over de Courtney. Then Wallis said, 'Shortly afterwards Lucy Walters disappeared from the village too, so I rather think she went with him, away from Abbeyford. All I hope is that they *stay* away!'

Adelina felt relief flood through her for Lynwood's sake.

At that moment three riders appeared out of the wood and rode across the open fields a short distance away. One horseman slowed down and drew apart from the others. He stopped and looked towards Adelina and Wallis Trent, their horses close together as they talked. He watched them for a few moments then spurred his horse, and, with the wild abandon of jealous rage, galloped madly away.

'Oh no!' Adelina whispered. 'That was Francis. Oh *no!*'

On her return to Lynwood Hall Adelina tried to seek out Lynwood, but he had shut himself in the library and posted a footman at the door with the strictest order—on pain of dismissal—that he was available to no one.

He did not appear for dinner, nor did he visit her room that night. Adelina sent a note to him, begging *'please let me explain'*, but there was no response.

The following morning Adelina found that Lord Lynwood had left early for London—without her!

Adelina hurried to Lady Lynwood's apartments. Without pausing to knock, she burst into the small room Lady Lynwood called her boudoir.

'How dare he go back to London without me? How dare he leave me stranded here?'

The old lady showed no surprise at Adelina's sudden, unheralded appearance, nor at her anger. An amused smile played upon her lips. 'It seems you haven't yet tethered him as securely as you thought, miss.'

The fire of Adelina's rage died and she sank miserably into a chair. 'What shall I do—what am I to do? He can't leave me—not *now!*' It was a cry of anguish from the heart.

Lady Lynwood eyed her shrewdly, seeming to be able to look deep into

Adelina's mind and read even her most secret fears. She nodded thoughtfully, then, appearing to come to a decision she said quietly, 'Then go after him, my dear.'

Adelina raised her head slowly. 'Go—after him?' she repeated dazedly.

'If I'm not much mistaken,' the Countess said briskly, 'you're in love with him, and—I think you have an even greater need of him now than ever before. Am I right?'

Adelina gasped and the colour flooded her face. 'How—did you know? How could you?'

'Women know these things, Adelina,' she nodded wisely, then she added with a snort of derision, 'but you cannot expect a *man* to guess. You'll have to tell him—then see what he'll do about it.'

'Yes, yes, I must tell him.'

'Come along then, girl, go and pack your belongings. We'll leave the day after tomorrow.'

The coach bumped and rattled over the rough roads until Adelina felt herself shaken limb from limb. So, as they reached the outskirts of the great sprawling city, Adelina was irritable and weary, though

Lady Lynwood seemed unruffled.

Towards evening the vehicle drew up outside Adelina's apartment. Tired and hungry and feeling dusty from so much travelling, what she most wanted was to fall into bed and sleep and sleep. But determination drove her on.

Lady Lynwood peered out of the coach as Adelina alighted. 'No doubt I shall be seeing you again shortly?'

'I guess you will, my lady,' Adelina said and, as she hurried up the steps to her apartment, she heard Lady Lynwood's laughter before the carriage rattled away over the cobblestones to her own home.

Some two hours later Adelina descended the staircase and entered a hired cab which she instructed to drive to Lynwood's Mayfair house.

The windows were ablaze with light and the sound of music met her as she alighted. Obviously Lynwood was entertaining and in great style.

When she entered the ballroom, there was, for a few seconds a stunned silence, swiftly followed by a babble of voices as everyone tried to appear disinterested.

Adelina's eyes scanned the dancing couples until she saw Lynwood. He was dancing with Helene Lyon! So, Adelina thought grimly, it had not taken him many hours to seek out his former mistress.

Lord Eversleigh and his wife, Madeleine, soon found their way to Adelina's side through the throng of people.

'Adelina, my dear,' Madeleine smiled revealing her ugly teeth. 'How good it is to see you again.'

'Well, my lord, are you going to dance with me?' she asked Eversleigh. His eyes met hers and he smiled. 'Delighted, madam,' he quipped and raised her hand gallantly to his lips. Adelina refused to see the hurt in Madeleine's eyes, her only thought was to make Lynwood jealous.

Adelina danced the whole night away, determined to captivate, to flirt, even to break a few hearts, but every moment she was aware of the time Lynwood spent with Helene Lyon.

Not until dawn did the guests begin to depart in their carriages. Adelina was exhausted. The long, wearisome journey followed by a night of merrymaking had taken their toll. Her aching limbs felt like lead and she could scarcely force her eyelids to stay open. But, doggedly, she refused to leave until she had spoken to Lynwood—and alone!

Breakfast was being served for those guests who still lingered. Adelina found a cold collation laid out in the dining-room and the guests were helping themselves in a casual and informal manner. There was much laughter and banter and a few malicious whisperings of the way Adelina and Helene had, by mutual silent consent, tried to ignore each other for the most part, and, when obliged to come face to face, had been icily polite.

Adelina sighed as she ate. There were still too many people about for her to speak to Francis in private and yet she could not leave the matter unresolved much longer.

Helene Lyon seemed to be making no preparations for her departure. It was as if each one were weighing up the odds, pitting her hold on Lynwood against the other.

Meanwhile, Lynwood seemed unconcerned. He sauntered amongst his guests, laughing and talking and when his glance rested upon either Adelina or Helene, there was the cynical half smile upon his lips.

At last Adelina could bear it no longer. Touching Lynwood lightly on the arm she said meekly, 'My lord, may I speak with you?'

'Of course, my dear,' Lynwood's eyes challenged hers, then lazily he scanned the whole of her body as if, mentally, he were seeing her in all her naked loveliness.

'What is it you want to say to me?'

'May we speak—in private?'

His eyes mocked her. 'Are you propositioning me, madam, before all my guests?' He laughed, and those nearby who had overheard the interchange of conversation, joined in the laughter.

Adelina felt her temper rising, but with a superb effort she willed herself to smile brightly and say, 'I think you will agree that what I have to say is best said in privacy, my lord.'

The laughter changed from mere amusement to ribald guffaws. 'Oho, Francis, what have you been about?'

'You'll have to choose now, Francis. I'll put my money on the red-haired filly against the black-haired mare!'

More shouts of laughter followed: 'I'll wager twenty to one on the mare.'

At once the room was a babble of noisy bantering. Adelina felt the colour rise in her cheeks. She felt insulted.

'Come, Adelina, let them have their fun at our expense. They mean no harm.' He took her arm and gently steered her through the throng to his study.

It was still quite dark and the room was only dimly lit by a candelabrum suspended from the ceiling. In the grate a cheerful log fire crackled, the flames leaping and dancing. It was a cosy, quiet room away from the noise and laughter. Lord Lynwood stood with his back to the fire, his feet set wide apart. His eyes were upon Adelina mockingly. 'Well, my dear, what is it you have to say to me which is of such importance that I must be dragged away from my guests?'

Suddenly, Adelina felt nervous. She had been so sure that her news would win him over to her, away from Helene Lyon again. Now that the moment of truth was here, she was not so certain. He seemed so remote from her somehow. She decided that a gentle, feminine humility was the best attitude to adopt. She would try to appeal to his protective instincts once more, for wasn't that how their relationship had begun? Even though now, for her part at least, it had grown to love.

She moved across the room and stood

close to him, looking up into his face, a tremulous smile upon her lips, her eyes brimming with unshed tears. 'Francis,' she said in a husky whisper. 'I am with child. Your child.'

She waited, watching the expression upon his face change from cynical amusement to shock and then there was that strange look of torment so often in his eyes and his mouth twisted cruelly.

'*My* child, madam? How can I be sure of that? How do I know it isn't Trent's brat?'

If he had struck her across the face with all his might it would not have hurt as much as his savage words did. Adelina gasped and her eyes were wide. 'Francis—I swear to you it's your child. You must believe me.'

'Must, madam? There's no *must* about it. I saw you talking to him that day. How do I know you haven't been meeting him in secret all the time we were at Lynwood Hall?'

Anger flashed in her green eyes and pride came to her rescue. 'How dare you even *think* that of me, Francis?' She whirled around and made for the door, but Lynwood caught hold of her. They stared at each other, so many emotions between them, pride, anger, love and passion—and even a little hatred!

Suddenly Lynwood's shoulders slumped. 'Oh, Adelina! Adelina!' he passed his hand wearily over his forehead. He put his arms about her and laid his cheek against her hair.

'Don't go, Adelina! It'll be—all right—I promise.'

Adelina sighed. His promise held no note of conviction. It seemed they could not find happiness together. And yet to be apart would bring them even greater torment!

CHAPTER 8

So their life slipped back into what it had been before Lord Lynwood's unfortunate duel with Thomas de Courtney. Society had taken both of them into its bosom again, for Adelina was to meet Mr de Courtney frequently at social gatherings and the onlookers—ignorant of previous events—would not have been aware that anything had ever been amiss.

Lynwood, despite his promise, continued to treat Adelina at times with love, at times with a calculated indifference and sometimes with almost hatred.

Adelina, confused by his weather-vane moods and in the final, emotional stages of pregnancy, for the first time in her life felt vulnerable and so alone.

More than ever she yearned for the security of her grandfather's love.

About two months before the expected date of her confinement, Lord Lynwood entered her boudoir shortly after breakfast. He held a letter in his hand.

'Adelina my dear. I have some bad news from Abbeyford.'

Her face turned pale and her hands fluttered nervously to her throat. 'Not—not my grandfather?'

'No—no. Emily. She—she died shortly after the birth of her son.'

'Oh I'm sorry. So very sorry. Poor Emily.'

'The child will live. He is to be called James.'

Lynwood stood watching her, as she turned her green eyes brimming with unshed tears towards him. 'Oh, Francis, is it so—dangerous to give birth? My mother and now Emily.'

He knelt beside her and put his own hand over hers in a gesture of tenderness. 'No—no, my dear. Don't fear. I shall see you have the best care. I promise.'

One evening towards the middle of October, Adelina felt the first twinge of labour pains. Lynwood was away from home so it was left to Jane to make all the arrangements for Adelina's confinement. Adelina was well advanced in labour when Lynwood returned home in the early hours of the following morning and was informed of the news by his butler. By the time he arrived at her apartment to see Adelina, all her conscious thought was so filled with pain that she was scarcely aware of his presence. The room was so hot and stifling. Faces wafted about her in a pain-ridden haze, voices shouted commands at her that she had no idea how to obey. The world was suddenly a hostile and frightening place. It was a nightmare of darkness, of a throbbing in her ears, of being tossed about in a violent storm. Strange, horrific pictures came before her eyes. The suffocating blackness, then, unbidden, Evan's face, cruelly twisted with passion and revenge.

'No—no,' her parched, cracked lips parted.

Then Lynwood's face, haggard and white with worry, was before her. Through her delirium she tried to reach out with trembling fingers to touch his face. But the mists closed in and his face faded from her sight.

Then there was pain again and a pulling and pushing and she felt as if her insides were being pulled from her. She screamed but once and then it was over. Somewhere, as if from a long way off, she heard the sound of a new-born baby yelling lustily. Faces came close to hers, mouthing words she heard but could not understand. Still they were pummelling her body as if, even yet, it was not all done. Finally, they left her in peace, washed and wrapped in clean linen. Exhausted, she slept.

It was not until much later that she awoke and realised that, except for a soreness, all the pain was gone. She moved her hands and felt the flatness of her stomach. She sighed. Then it was over. She turned her head and found herself looking into Francis's eyes. For a long moment they regarded each other solemnly. He saw a woman with her fine auburn hair strewn across the pillow, her face pale and her eyes with deep smudges of blue beneath them, telling of her suffering, and yet she was still beautiful, and damn it, he thought irritated with himself, still desirable!

Adelina observed Frances. He was unshaven, with a shadow of stubble upon his face, his eyes were weary, his hair ruffled, his shirt open at the neck. She guessed he had been sitting beside her bed, dozing and waking and watching over her. But there was still a remoteness about him, a bitter twist to his mouth and a hurt look deep in his blue eyes.

She smiled tremulously, but he did not return her smile. A new fear struck her. Perhaps there was something amiss—something wrong with the baby, or even with her! Perhaps she, too, like her mother and Emily, was going to die!

'Francis?' she whispered. 'The baby?'

He leaned forward and after a moment's hesitation he said, 'You have a daughter, Adelina.'

'She—is she—healthy?'

'She is healthy, though not particularly beautiful. But, then, what newborn babes are?' His tone was bitter with disappointment. Hours earlier he had looked upon the baby, eagerly searching for some likeness to himself. But the child's hair was black and her skin dark, whereas Lynwood's hair and skin were fair!

Sick at heart he had turned away. Wallis Trent had black hair and a swarthy skin. The picture of Adelina and Wallis Trent talking together merged with that other image of his adored Caroline running into the arms of Thomas Cole.

'And me? What about me?' Adelina was saying.

'You?' There was a harsh note in his voice, a cruel tone. 'You, madam, are in excellent health. The doctor said he rarely saw an easier birth.'

Adelina smiled with wry amusement. 'Perhaps it was—from where he was standing!' She twisted her head upon the pillow and looked into Lynwood's face. 'Why did you say "you have a daughter?" She's your daughter as well.'

'Is she?' Still the doubt was there.

Adelina tried to raise herself on one elbow but found the effort too painful. 'Why don't you believe me? I wouldn't lie to you over a thing like that?'

But the painful memories, seen through the uncomprehending eyes of boyhood, had warped the emotions he had carried forward into manhood. He could not allow himself to trust Caroline's daughter!

If they stayed together, Lynwood thought, if he married her even, there was no hope of happiness and contentment for them while this jealousy and distrust ate at him like a canker. Yet, if he sent her away, his life would be empty and a lonely misery.

She was looking at him now, her green eyes beseeching him, but he hardened his heart against her silent plea.

'Well, madam,' he stood up and walked to the end of the bed. 'I am glad you are safely delivered of your child and that both of you are healthy, but I must make it clear that I have no intention of marrying you—not now or ever!'

Adelina trembled. 'Oh, Francis. You can't mean to allow your daughter to go through life with the stigma of being a bastard. You could not be so cruel to an innocent child?'

Lynwood flinched, but he set his jaw in a hard, unyielding line and said slowly and deliberately, 'I will not marry you, Adelina. I—cannot!' He came close to the bed and, looking down at her he said through clenched teeth, 'If you had been a virgin when you came to me, or if your child had been a boy, then I might—I just might—have married you!'

It took some seconds for the full impact of his words to strike her. Then her hopes crumpled. Never had she loved him as much as she did at this moment, when he turned his back resolutely upon her and walked out of the room—and out of her life!

Some while later Jane came into the room.

'Oh, madam, what is it?' she asked sympathetically, putting her arm around Adelina's shaking shoulders. 'Don't fret so. The baby's fine. She's a beauty. Nurse will be bringing her along to see you soon.'

'Nurse?'

'Why yes, didn't his lordship tell you? He's engaged one of the best dry-nurses in London. Rumour has it she's been nurse to a duke's children. She's a bit old and very strict with all of us, but she's as gentle as a lamb when she holds the baby. Then, of course there's the wet-nurse.'

'Well, you can send *her* away. No one

but me is going to suckle my child,' Adelina declared.

Jane's mouth dropped open in surprise, but she made no comment. After a few moments she said, 'By the way, madam, what are you going to call the dear little thing?'

Adelina dried her eyes and blew her nose. Anger made her stop weeping. 'I don't know.' She paused then asked, 'What's the equivalent of Francis for a girl?'

'Well, there's Frances, but I think it's spelt differently, but I'm not right good at spelling, ma'am.'

Adelina nodded. 'Yes, with an "e" instead of an 'i'. Can you think of any more?'

Jane wrinkled her brow and thought. 'The only other one I can think of, ma'am, is Francesca.'

'Francesca,' Adelina repeated the name and thought for a moment and then nodded. 'Yes, I like it. I'll call her Francesca Caroline. My mother's name was Caroline.'

She did not see Lynwood again, but he made lavish and generous arrangements for the care of the baby—whether or not he really believed the child to be his. As soon as she felt well enough, Adelina made preparations to leave London.

And there was only one place she could go.

Adelina was returning to Abbeyford.

She travelled by stage-coach, taking only Jane with her to care for the child. The nurse, engaged by Lynwood, was dismissed.

The journey was a nightmare. The baby, Francesca, became sick. The horses were old and tired and travelled at only five miles or so an hour. The journey seemed endless and took three days instead of two. The cold seeped into their bones and once all the passengers were obliged to alight from the coach at a particularly steep hill, for the horses could not pull the loaded coach up the hill.

'I hope we don't have an accident, ma'am,' Jane said, panting along at the side of Adelina who carried the baby. 'I reckon this coachman's not to be trusted. Strikes me he's overloaded the coach.'

Adelina said nothing, but bit down hard upon her lower lip and held the child closer to her against the winter wind.

After what seemed weeks instead of

days, bruised and battered through being tossed about in the rattling coach, they arrived near Amberly. Hiring a local cab, Adelina took a bold step. 'Lynwood Hall, please, driver,' she instructed him.

Jane gasped and looked at Adelina with wide eyes. 'Oh, ma'am. Ought we to?'

'Just for the present, Jane, until I've had time to look around.'

Adelina did not take her maidservant into her confidence, but she intended to stay at Lynwood Hall just long enough to find out, once and for all, whether she could be reconciled with her grandfather. If not, then she would return to America.

Their arrival at Lynwood Hall caused little stir. Lady Lynwood, who had seen no reason to remain in London during Adelina's necessary absence from Society, had returned earlier to her country home. Now, as she greeted Adelina, she seemed amused by the situation. Her laughter cackled readily. 'Well, miss, you didn't manage to lead him to the altar, then? Hmm—I'm surprised. I thought he loved you.' Her sharp eyes scanned Adelina's face. 'And you him.'

Adelina remained silent.

'Have you had news of your relatives

while you've been in London?' Lady Lynwood asked suddenly.

'Only—only about Emily.'

'Martha Langley has been very ill. Just after Emily's death. She is partially paralysed. Her husband's at his wit's end to know how to cope with her.' Her beady eyes looked straight at Adelina. 'Shall you go and see them?'

Adelina shrugged. 'I doubt if I'd be welcomed.'

'I think in their present pitiable state, they'd welcome the Devil himself, if he offered help.'

'Well,' Adelina hesitated. 'I'll have to think about it.'

Two days later, however, when her small daughter had recovered from the harassing journey and was once again a happy, gurgling infant, Adelina, driving herself and dressed warmly, took the gig from Lord Lynwood's stables and set out towards Abbeyford.

It was early January 1818, and her heart lifted as she drove along the narrow lanes. She found the frosty, country air invigorating after city life. As she drove through Amberly, Adelina scarcely glanced at the villagers, remembering their previous hostility. Children scuttled out of the way of her horse's flying hooves and mothers scooped up their toddlers to safety. Just as she left the village she passed by a small cottage set a little apart from the other dwellings and standing some distance back from the road. A barefoot toddler, with a dirty face, bright red curls and a ragged shirt, tottered down the path, and briefly she saw a man emerging from the cottage doorway. She was past so quickly and he was some way from her that she could not really recognise him, yet there was something vaguely familiar about the stocky build and broad shoulders. But she knew no one in Amberly, she told herself. For some inexplicable reason the sight of the shadowy figure had awakened in her a feeling of unease. Then she whipped up the horse towards Abbeyford and forgot all about the man and his red-haired child.

As she emerged from the trees she pulled on the reins and drew the horse to a halt. She sat for a moment, drinking in the scene before her. Immediately below her was Abbeyford Manor, then farther down the valley she followed the twisting lane with her eyes, catching sight of the ford and the tiny footbridge and then the village itself with the church in its midst and, close by, the Vicarage and, far beyond on the opposite hill, was Abbeyford Grange where her grandfather lived in self-imposed loneliness. To her right were the abbey ruins and all around lay the farmlands belonging to Lord Royston.

Adelina slapped the reins and her horse trotted on obediently. She took the narrow lane towards Abbeyford village and was soon turning in the Vicarage gates.

The story Lady Lynwood had told Adelina about Mrs Langley proved to be true. She was in a pitiable state and Mr Langley was thin and ill with worry and the burden of caring for his truculent wife.

The door was opened to Adelina by the maid and when she was shown into the Vicar's study, Adelina gasped to see the change in him. His hair was now completely snow-white but ruffled and unkempt. He had always stooped slightly, but now his shoulders were hunched more than ever. His face was gaunt and his eyes ringed with dark shadows from lack of sleep. His yellowy skin was loose and pouchy as if he had suddenly lost weight. His clothes, hanging untidily on him, were blotched with stains.

His eyes widened as he realised who his visitor was. 'Adelina my dear. How glad I am to see you.' The tears welled in his eyes, and Adelina was moved to bend and kiss his forehead. As she followed the Vicar's shambling steps into the drawing-room, Adelina noticed the thick film of dust everywhere.

She stepped into the room. Sitting in a chair near the fire was Mrs Langley—a mere shadow of the formidable woman Adelina remembered. She seemed shrunken and wasted away. Her hands, lying uselessly in her lap, twitched from time to time. She breathed noisily through her mouth, which hung open. Her eyes turned towards Adelina and there was a flash of recognition in them. There was bitterness and venom in her eyes, but, though she worked her mouth, Martha Langley could no longer give vent to her feelings with her tongue.

For all her dislike of this woman, Adelina felt sorry for her. She sat down opposite her and forced herself to smile at Mrs Langley.

'She knows you, Adelina, and she understands what we say to her. Her comprehension is quite unimpaired,' Mr Langley explained. 'It's purely—physical.'

Adelina nodded. 'I'm truly sorry to see you like this, ma'am, believe me.'

Mrs Langley gave a loud sniff and Adelina almost laughed aloud. She hadn't forgotten how to give that famous sniff which in itself could speak volumes!

Swiftly, Adelina made up her mind. 'Mrs Langley—you need help, don't you? And I need somewhere to stay—just for a few weeks.'

Mrs Langley made some weird noises and her head rocked from side to side.

'No—no, I know you don't like me—never have, and I know what you must think of me now. But for once you're going to have to forget your pride for your husband's sake. Just look at him. He'll be ill next if he goes on much longer the way he is.'

Mrs Langley's eyes swivelled to look at him, then, giving a peculiar sort of strangulated groan, she closed her eyes and rocked her whole being to and fro.

'That's settled then,' Adelina said, standing up. 'We'll be moving in within the next few days.'

'We?' Mr Langley questioned.

'Er—yes. Myself, my maid and—er—the baby.'

'Baby!' He was obviously startled, and Mrs Langley began to make a gurgling noise, which Adelina ignored.

'Yes,' she said, as casually as she could manage. 'Didn't you know I have a baby daughter. She's three months old.'

'Adelina!' There was a world of sadness and disappointment in his tone. 'Oh, Adelina—how could you?'

He paused and then said slowly, as if battling with himself. 'Well—I don't know what to say about that. I'm sure. I mean...'

'Look, you need help—desperately. And now poor Emily's gone...' She saw him flinch at the mention of his daughter, but Adelina continued with a little of the ruthlessness that had been her mother's nature. 'There's only me left to come and help out a while. Now don't let pride stand in your way. By the look of both of you, you could sure use a little help right now.'

She paused while he appeared to be struggling with his conscience. Quietly, she said, 'I really don't think you have any choice, have you?'

He sighed. 'I suppose not.'

Within a few days Adelina had packed her trunks once more and taken leave of Lynwood Hall.

'So,' Lady Lynwood had remarked drily, 'you're going to play nursemaid for a while, are you, miss?' She laughed. 'You'll soon tire of that I don't doubt and be back knocking on our door.'

'No,' Adelina said quietly with infinite sadness. 'I can never ask another favour of Lord Lynwood.'

'Really?' The old lady raised her eyebrows sceptically. 'Mmm—well, we'll see.'

'If I have to leave Abbeyford again, I shall go back to America.'

Lady Lynwood showed surprise at Adelina's remark. Adelina turned her clear green eyes upon the old lady, whom she had come to regard with affection. 'There's only one thing I want now other than...' she stopped, unable to speak Lynwood's name. 'Only one thing—to meet my grandfather. If—if that is not possible, then—then there is nothing else I can do.'

'Don't waste your life waiting for a stupid old man to overcome his hurt pride—or for that matter,' she added, referring to her own son, 'a stupid *young* one!'

Surprisingly, Adelina's way of life back at the Vicarage bore little resemblance to the previous time. Mr Langley, worn out by the unaccustomed domestic burden, was only too thankful to relinquish the reins to Adelina, who soon had the servants performing their duties properly instead of idly taking advantage of the elderly, mild-tempered Vicar. Mrs Langley was completely helpless physically, nor could she voice her disapproval. Only her eyes showed the resentment she still felt towards Adelina.

'It won't be for long,' Adelina comforted herself.

When the house had been restored to some sort of order and Mr Langley sufficiently recovered to take up his parish duties once more, and Francesca had settled to a routine and began to thrive in the country air, Adelina decided it was time she visited Abbeyford Grange.

One particularly warm and spring-like day in early March Adelina left the Vicarage and the village and took the footpath through the open fields until she came to the small footbridge crossing the stream. She stood on the bridge, her hand resting on the rail and looked up at Abbeyford Grange. Her heart began to beat faster as she walked up the slope towards the high wall surrounding the house and garden. Reaching the wall she found a door and, twisting the heavy ring, she pushed it open and stepped into the sunken garden. Her gaze was drawn to the house—the house which had been her mother's home. It looked empty, deserted almost, although she knew Lord Royston still lived here, no doubt with several servants. But the house had a desolate air, an atmosphere of decay and neglect.

Without realising she had moved, she found herself in a square in the centre of the rose garden and when a voice spoke close by, Adelina jumped violently.

'No need to ask who *you* are.'

Adelina turned to see an old man sitting on a garden seat, a rug wrapped warmly over his knees. His face was wrinkled and his bushy white eyebrows almost met in the centre of his forehead as he frowned. His head was bald, except for a white tuft of hair over each ear. His hand held a walking-stick, the gnarled knuckles showing white as he gripped the stick and from time to time he struck the ground with it.

This was Lord Royston—her grandfather!

'No tongue in your head?' he growled, as Adelina continued to stare at him. His reprimand made her hold her head higher—proud and defiant.

'Goodday, my lord.'

'Oh, sit down, sit down, now you're here,' he said irritably.

Obediently, she sat beside him on the seat, half turned towards him.

'Well—am I what you expected?' The eyebrows rose and fell.

Adelina laughed. 'Not really.'

'Hmm,' he grunted.

'How do you know who I am?' she asked.

'Because you're the image of your mother,' he muttered and thumped his stick on the ground.

'Oh—I'm sorry.'

'Sorry? Why be sorry? She was a lovely girl—a lovely girl.'

'I'm sorry because I must bring back painful memories for you.'

'Why did she do it? Why—why?' Again

the stick thumped the ground as he voiced aloud the question which had haunted him for over twenty years.

'I can't remember things clearly because I was only nine when she died.'

'So long ago and I didn't even know she was dead until you first came to Abbeyford,' the old man murmured and he seemed to shrink a little more.

'But I can recall little things,' Adelina went on. 'I can remember the happiness in our house when I was little, the warmth and the love. I believe she and my father were devoted to each other.'

'Was he good to her?'

'Yes—yes, I think he was. After she died—he—well—he ceased to care, even for me. He took to drinking and gambling. He lost his job, we lost our home. Not immediately, of course, but over the years we lost everything until we had to move from the plantation in South Carolina to New York, to the poorest, roughest neighbourhood.' Why, she thought, am I blurting all this out within moments of meeting him?

'You say your father ceased to care for you. Did—did he ill-treat you?'

'No,' Adelina shrugged and smiled

sadly, remembering. 'But the roles were reversed. I looked after him. I became the strong one. I had to be, to survive. That's why I'm so sure he loved my mother. When she died, he just stopped living too.'

There was silence between them while the embittered old man struggled to understand. At last he sighed. 'Ah, well, I suppose none of it is your fault anyway. Perhaps I was not entirely blameless. I was trying to arrange a marriage for her to a man she obviously did not love. That locket round your neck...?' he asked suddenly.

'It was my mother's—she always wore it and I have worn it ever since I was—given it.'

'Open it,' he commanded. As she did so, he leant forward to look at the two tiny likenesses enclosed within. Slowly, he nodded. 'Yes—that's the locket I gave her on the very same day she ran away. And she wore it all the time?'

Adelina nodded. 'Yes. She loved you dearly, but she loved my father too and couldn't bear to spend her life without him, even though he wasn't your choice. I'm sure she didn't mean to hurt you so.

I think she really thought that, once they were married and I was born, you would forgive them.'

'It seems—I left it too late. But I could,' the old man added with surprising briskness, 'make it up to you. Would you care to come up to the house?'

Adelina's lips parted as she drew breath sharply and her green eyes shone with happiness. Then her delight faded.

'Grandfather—there's something you should know. I—I have a child.'

'So—I have a great-grandchild, have I?' The old man began to smile.

'But,' she blurted out. 'I'm not married. My child is illegitimate.'

Lord Royston was still, his face immobile. 'I see,' he said flatly. 'I wonder I hadn't heard.'

'Your servants would know, but I guess none of them dared to tell you.'

'And the father?'

Adelina hesitated then said bluntly. 'Francis—Lord Lynwood.'

'Lynwood! My God!' For a moment his face was contorted with disbelief, then he sighed heavily. 'Lynwood!' He repeated incredulously. 'Of all people—Lynwood!'

He recovered himself a little and turned

his sharp eyes upon her. 'And he won't marry you?'

Sadly Adelina shook her head. 'No.'

'But you love him?'

'Yes,' Adelina whispered. 'Yes, I do. And I thought he—he cared for me but—but...' the unfinished sentence lay between them. There was some reason why Lynwood would not marry her, some reason she could not understand.

'You're too like your mother!' Lord Royston said bluntly.

Adelina gasped. 'I don't understand. What has that to do with it?'

'Don't you know?'

Slowly Adelina shook her head.

'As a boy, Francis idolised your mother, followed her about his eyes always on her. Then suddenly, I remember, he held himself aloof, remote from her. He seemed to pass from boyhood to manhood in the space of a day. Very soon afterwards she ran away with Thomas Cole and I believe—though I never had any proof—that Francis learnt of her—her affair—perhaps even saw them together and was hurt—deeply.'

He turned to look straight into Adelina's eyes. 'I realise you cannot be expected to understand, but what your mother did was a shocking thing. She deceived me, she risked her reputation and she married below her—good and honourable though Thomas Cole may have been,' he added swiftly, as Adelina opened her mouth to defend her father. 'They came from such different worlds—it could never have worked.'

'But it *did* work. They were happy—I know they were, until she died.'

Lord Royston smiled sadly. 'You have your mother's spirit, I see. But Caroline was too spoilt, too selfish. Eventually life with Thomas Cole would not have been enough for her.'

'I suppose we can never know that really, can we?' Adelina said.

'No, my dear, not now.' He patted her hand. 'At least, if she was happy for a while, that's something. And, knowing my wilful daughter, she would never, ever, have admitted she'd been wrong anyway.' Suddenly his eyes twinkled with a merriment long buried. 'Any more than *I'm* likely to admit I could have been wrong. You've a stubborn old man for a grandfather, my dear.'

She smiled at him. 'So I see,' she said

impishly, the happiness flooding through her. He was not going to turn her away.

At last, Adelina had come home.

Together they rose and she put her arm through his and slowly they walked towards the house.

Unobserved by either of them, a man on a jet black horse stood beneath the shadow of a huge elm tree at the main gate, watching the slow progress of the old man and the young woman, arm in arm, their heads bent close to each other.

Stealthily, Wallis Trent turned his horse away and cantered down the hill.

CHAPTER 9

So one of Adelina's dearest wishes had come true—she had found her grandfather and their mutual joy in each other helped to ease her sense of loss over Lynwood.

She asked nothing of Lord Royston and he offered nothing, but each was happy in their closeness. He even accepted her child and the sight of the old man with the baby on his knee made Adelina's heart fill with love.

One afternoon, driving the small gig her grandfather had insisted she borrow from his stables whenever she wished, Adelina took a drive along the narrow lanes. Returning to the Grange, she rounded a corner and almost collided with Wallis Trent on his huge black stallion. Wallis pulled on his reins so hard that Jupiter reared and Adelina pulled hard to the right and her horse and gig ran into the steep bank bordering the lane. The small vehicle tipped sideways and Adelina screamed as she fell to the ground. For a moment the gig hung suspended and then slowly it toppled right over. Adelina screamed again, a piercing shriek of pain as the gig fell upon her legs.

Wallis was already down from his horse and running towards her as it fell, but too late to prevent it. The weight was only heavy on her for a few seconds, for he immediately grasped the gig and with his great strength lifted it clear of her.

'Can you pull yourself free, Adelina?' Wallis asked.

'I think so,' she gasped and dragged herself along the grass until she was clear. Wallis, grunting with exertion, heaved and pushed until the gig was almost upright then he shouted a command to the horse, which had been brought down when the vehicle toppled over. 'Up, boy, come on,' and he clicked encouragingly. The horse struggled valiantly to get to its feet and at the same time Wallis righted the gig. Then he turned swiftly to Adelina.

'Adelina—are you hurt?' He knelt beside her, concern on his handsome face.

'It's my right leg.'

'Keep still,' he commanded and placed gentle fingers upon her leg, searching to see if a bone might be broken.

'Ouch!' Adelina cried in pain as he touched a tender spot just below her knee.

'I don't think there's anything broken, my dear,' Wallis said, 'but your leg's no doubt badly bruised. Whatever were you doing driving so recklessly along a narrow lane?' His tone took on a note of severity. 'You are lucky to escape with slight injury!'

'If it comes to that,' Adelina said crossly, rubbing her leg, 'what were you doing galloping along the lane? You were going every bit as fast as me!'

Wallis frowned. 'Well—perhaps I was.'

He stood up. 'See if you can stand, Adelina. Here, take my hand.'

Carefully, she stood up. Though she could feel her leg was badly bruised and she was feeling very shaken from the incident, there were certainly no bones broken.

'I'm quite all right, thank you,' Adelina said stiffly, and tried to pull her hand away from his, but he held her fast. Surprised, she looked up into his face. He was looking down at her now with an expression which she had never expected to see in Wallis Trent's cold eyes.

'My dear Adelina,' his deep voice was soft. 'I can't tell you how glad I am to see you again.'

Adelina almost laughed aloud at the contrast between this greeting and the last occasion, but she held herself in check and merely allowed herself a small smile.

'Are you well, Mr Trent?'

'I am—and I'm thankful to see you're not hurt. Let me help you into the gig. I'll tether Jupiter to the rear and drive you home.'

'Oh, that won't be necessary. I am quite able to drive myself...'

'Nonsense, I won't hear of it,' Wallis

said with authority.

Minutes later the gig was moving through the country lanes once more, this time with Wallis Trent at the reins and Adelina close beside him on the narrow seat.

As they passed by a group of workmen, going home at the end of their day's work, Adelina caught a fleeting glimpse of the grim, resentful expressions upon their faces. Where recently she had begun to be greeted with courtesy and friendliness by the villagers, now their hostility was plain to see.

She glanced thoughtfully at the man beside her. It was not she herself they resented, but the man in whose company they saw her!

Wallis Trent was a hated man!

He drove through the village and took the lane back to the Grange. 'I was delighted to learn of your reconciliation with your grandfather, my dear.'

'Oh, so you've heard?' Immediately she knew the reason for the swift change in his attitude towards her, for his sudden friendliness.

'News of any sort always travels fast in a small community but, of course, on this occasion,' he added loftily, 'I heard it from

Lord Royston himself.'

'Really?' Adelina frowned slightly. She was not aware that Wallis Trent had seen her grandfather recently. She wondered if he was telling the truth.

'I'll just pay my respects to Lord Royston,' he was saying as he helped her from the gig. But it seemed that her grandfather was not as pleased to see him as Wallis Trent would have her believe.

'What are you doing here, Trent? Not your day to come for another week.'

Wallis explained their accidental meeting.

'Hmm,' the old man growled. 'Well—now you're here, sit down, sit down.'

His old eyes searched for Adelina and softened at the sight of her as she moved forward to kiss his cheek. His knarled hand clasped hers and he looked up into her face.

Thoughtfully, Wallis Trent watched the affectionate scene.

Wallis Trent became a frequent visitor to the Vicarage, where Adelina and her daughter still lived. He insisted he should accompany Adelina whenever she took a drive or a walk. He brought small gifts for the baby and saw to it that whatever was needed at the Vicarage was provided immediately. As the summer passed, he became more and more attentive.

Adelina had no doubt as to the reason behind Wallis Trent's sudden friendship, almost courtship. Since her reconciliation with Lord Royston, she knew Wallis would believe the old man had now made Adelina his heiress. But she did not think that even Wallis Trent had the gall to admit this fact openly. She was to be proved wrong!

One evening he came to the Vicarage and asked Adelina if they might talk privately. She took him into the drawing-room, seated herself before the fire and waited for him to speak. Wallis stood in front of the fireplace and looked down at her.

'Adelina—during the past few weeks and months we have spent a deal of time in each other's company and we seem compatible. I—in my position in the county and with a young son—have need of a wife. You...' he paused momentarily as if the subject which he must touch upon was abhorrent to him. 'Have need of a husband and a father for your daughter.'

Adelina remained silent, but her fingers were laced tightly together until the knuckles showed white.

'I must presume that Lynwood has not offered you marriage, or you would not have arrived back in Abbeyford.'

Adelina swallowed hard and fought back the tears which threatened as Wallis's words brought back vividly her memories of Lynwood.

With her new-found joy in her closeness with her grandfather, Adelina had resolutely told herself she was happy, that she now had what she had most wanted. But at this moment—in the midst of what was obviously a proposal of marriage from Wallis Trent—desolation and longing for Lynwood swept over her. The sight of his face, the feel of his arms about her. Her sense of loss was a physical ache.

'And so, my dear,' Wallis was saying, 'I am asking you to become my wife. I think you will agree that the arrangement would be of advantage to us both. It would also solve any dilemma Lord Royston may now feel.'

'Lord Royston?' Adelina pretended deliberately not to understand, wanting to force the words from Wallis's own lips.

'Well, my dear,' Wallis Trent straightened his back and thrust out his chest.

'You know that my wife, Emily, was Lord Royston's heiress?'

'Yes.'

'Since her death his lordship has entailed his estate to our son, Jamie. Now,' he shrugged and laughed and spread his hands expansively, 'you must see that with your recent reconciliation the old man must feel—well—torn between his obligation to keep his promise to my son and his—quite natural—new-found affection for you.'

With difficulty Adelina kept her face straight. Without the least desire for material gain, she found the whole absurd situation vastly amusing.

'And you think our marriage would safely ensure that the estate still comes to your son?'

Swiftly, he reassured her but his words lacked sincerity. 'My dear, I wouldn't want you to think that that was the sole purpose behind my proposal. Dear me, no! But, nevertheless, it is a consideration, a quite usual consideration among marriages in our Society. Though as an American you may not fully understand.'

'Oh, I think I do,' Adelina said wryly.

'Well, then, my dear, what is your answer?'

'Wallis—I, too, will be utterly frank. I do not love you, but I do love my daughter dearly and for her sake, and her sake alone, I will agree to become your wife.'

Resolutely, Adelina banished all thought of Lynwood's beloved face from her mind. For the sake of her baby daughter she ought to marry and, since there was no chance of Lynwood ever proposing to her, then she must accept Wallis Trent, even though she shuddered at the mere thought of being tied to this cold, ambitious man. Adelina loved her baby daughter ferociously and she would sacrifice all her own hopes of happiness to ensure her child's future and the security of a kind of legitimacy.

So Adelina agreed to marry Wallis Trent and the date of their marriage was set for New Year's Day.

On Christmas Day, a carriage drew into the Vicarage drive. A fine carriage bearing the Lynwood crest.

Lord Lynwood stepped down from it and stood looking at the house for a moment, as if still considering whether he should approach the door, or get back into his carriage and drive away.

At last, he climbed the steps slowly and

pulled on the bell-chord.

Adelina, who had seen his arrival, greeted him herself. It had taken a few moments for her to compose herself before opening the door, and although she managed to meet his eyes calmly, inside herself she was quivering with joy and fear and longing at the sight of him. She could see the sadness in his eyes as he gazed at her. He had struggled for days against coming, for to his mind it would show weakness on his part. It would appear as if he could not live without sight of her. And Francis, Earl of Lynwood, was not a man who liked to appear weak.

But the anguish in his heart had at last overcome his pride. He had found that, since Adelina had left him, he was obsessed by memories of her. Now, as he stood before her, still he could not say all the tender endearments which were in his heart. He merely said brusquely. 'I've come to bring the child some presents.' He could not even say 'my daughter'.

Adelina smiled, though still a little uncertainly. 'It's good to see you, Francis. And very kind of you to think of Francesca. Please come in.'

She led the way into the morning room.

Francis paused in the doorway as his glance fell upon the child playing on the rug. The infant raised her brilliant blue eyes to look at the stranger, then her face broke into a cherubic beam and she gurgled at him, holding out her chubby arms invitingly. Completely bemused, Lord Lynwood knelt before the child. Wonderingly, he reached out his fingers to touch her golden curls and gazed into her blue eyes so like his own. 'But—but she—her hair was—*black!*' he murmured.

'At first—yes. But a new-born baby's hair can change colour,' Adelina laughed, completely unaware of Lynwood's inner conflict. 'That black fuzz soon rubbed off. She was almost bald for a time and then her hair grew fair—and curly.'

Francesca reached out and grasped Lynwood's finger, pulling it towards her mouth.

'Mind,' Adelina warned. 'She's cutting teeth—she'll give you a nip.'

Francis said softly. 'Oh, we can stand that, my little love, can't we?'

The baby chuckled and chewed happily upon his finger. Never taking his eyes from the child, Francis said, 'Ask my coachman to bring in the parcels, please, Adelina?'

'Parcels?'

'Yes. Christmas gifts. Didn't you know, it's all the rage in London? The Duchess of York started it. She decorates her dining-room and piles it high with presents and invites not only her family and friends in but all her servants and many local children, and each one receives a gift.'

A few moments later the sofa-table was piled high with boxes of various shapes. With a smile of genuine pleasure, Lynwood reached for some of the parcels and placed them on the rug near Francesca. The baby's eyes grew round with wonder and her fingers touched the boxes.

'I think you'll have to help her open then,' Adelina said.

'There are some for you too,' Lynwood murmured, his attention still wholly upon the child.

Some little time later the room was littered with discarded wrappings and Francesca surrounded by numerous toys.

There was a rocking-horse with baby foot-rests: a doll's house complete with intricately made furniture and three tiny dolls, father, mother and baby each dressed in the fashion of the day. There were two bigger dolls, one a rag doll and one with a wax, painted face attached to a stuffed body. There was a jumping-jack, a ball, a drum and a rattle.

Adelina was still exclaiming with delight over her gifts from Lynwood. Impulsively, she threw her arms around his neck and kissed him on the mouth. 'Oh, thank you, Francis, you are generous.'

He slipped his arm around her waist. 'It's good to see you happy, my dear. Adelina...' He seemed about to say more, but at that moment the door opened and Wallis entered the room.

He stopped short as the picture of Adelina and Lord Lynwood in each other's arms met his eyes and Adelina's joy died instantly. In her happiness at seeing Lynwood again she had completely forgotten Wallis Trent!

'Francis has brought some wonderful gifts for Francesca, isn't it kind of him?' she explained. 'He says it's all the rage in London now.'

The two men eyed each other warily, dark anger upon Wallis Trent's face, while the bitterness and jealousy once more flooded through Lynwood's heart.

'You must know, my lord,' Wallis said

tersely, 'that I cannot allow Adelina to accept your gifts.'

Now anger flared in Lynwood's handsome face too. 'I beg your pardon...?'

'You will allow me to be the judge of that, Wallis,' Adelina said boldly. Wallis turned his scowling face upon her.

'Adelina—you have agreed to become my wife in a week's time. You will oblige me by obeying my wishes.'

Defiantly, Adelina raised her head higher and met Wallis's cold, hard eyes, at the same time she was acutely aware of the misery on Lynwood's face.

'When I become your wife—I will obey you. But this once, at least, you must allow Lord Lynwood to give the child his gifts. After all—*she is his daughter!*'

'Madam, by next week, legally, she will be my daughter, and he will have no claim upon her.'

'Married?' Lynwood said softly, turning towards Adelina. 'You are to marry Trent?'

Adelina closed her eyes in momentary overwhelming anguish. When she opened them again, Lynwood's face was a closed mask of indifference. 'Then it is as I thought—all the time,' he said bitterly, 'and to think I came here today hoping...

Ahh!' he let out a groan of utter rejection and dismissal.

As he turned to leave, Adelina stretched out her hands towards him. 'Francis!' she cried from the very depths of her being. *'Francis!'*

But Wallis caught hold of her and prevented her from following Lynwood. She heard the front door slam, heard the carriage move away, the sounds of its wheels growing fainter and knew that this time Lynwood would never return.

Adelina tore herself from Wallis's grasp and ran from the room, upstairs, to throw herself on her bed and give way to a paroxysm of weeping.

The marriage of Wallis Trent and Adelina Cole took place at eight-thirty on the morning of the first of January 1819. The only people present were Mr Langley, as officiating clergyman, Squire Guy Trent and his wife, and one or two of the Trents' employees.

There was to be no honeymoon, and Adelina, her child and her maid moved their belongings to Abbeyford Manor that same afternoon. Francesca was taken to the nursery wing to be cared for, along with

Jamie Trent, Wallis's son, by the nanny and the nursery maid. Jane was retained as Adelina's personal maid.

At the Vicarage, Adelina had dismissed the indolent servants who had been of little help to Mr Langley in his wife's illness and had persuaded Sarah Smithson to come back, this time as housekeeper. Adelina was sorry for the desperately unhappy, work-worn woman, who had lived her life sorrowing for a love that could not be, living with a man whose bitterness and resentment festered and grew over the years and was carried on by his stepson who had sworn revenge upon the Trents.

Adelina could not help but see that she was perhaps following the very same path as Sarah Smithson, for was not she marrying one man in order to give her illegitimate child a name, while still loving the father of her child? Just as Sarah Smithson had been obliged to do.

So a routine was established at Abbeyford Manor, but it was an existence without purpose for Adelina, a life which held little hope for the future. She found solace in her love for her daughter and her grandfather, but between herself and her husband there was a coldness, a remoteness. They had separate bedrooms and, though he visited her at night occasionally, his lovemaking was accomplished as if it were an act of duty, or a physical need which must be satisfied. No word of love or affection ever passed his lips. There was no tender wooing, no moments of joy and intimate laughter between them.

Lynwood, for all that his jealousy and distrust had over-shadowed their complete happiness, at least he had cared for her. Only now, living with the selfish, arrogant Wallis Trent, did Adelina realise how great her loss of Lynwood had been!

Adelina found that there was little for her to do in her new role at the Manor for Louisa Trent was still the mistress. Wallis entertained occasionally, but not often. From time to time she would accompany him as he rode around the estate, but she found the sullen, hostile stares of the workmen unnerving. Where before she could have been sure of a smile from the village folk, now all sign of friendliness from them was gone, because she had married the man they feared and disliked.

Strangely, her one adult companion at

Abbeyford Manor proved to be Squire Guy Trent. Between the lonely man and the young bride of a marriage of convenience there grew an affinity, an understanding born of a mutual loss and loneliness.

'There's a horse-dealer coming this afternoon,' Squire Trent told her one morning. 'Get Wallis to buy you a horse—then we could go for rides together.'

'Oh—I don't know,' Adelina hesitated. 'I don't like to ask...'

'Then it's time you did.' His bleary eyes were upon her face. 'You're a lovely girl, Adelina. My son doesn't realise how fortunate he is.'

Adelina smiled. 'I'll come and see the horses—I promise.'

That afternoon she found her way to the Squire's study, knocked sharply and then opened the door. A cloud of cigar smoke and the smell of whisky met her. She blinked as the smoke stung her eyes. Two men sat at the huge desk, the Squire and a stranger—a thin, shrewish little man with hollowed cheeks and shifty eyes.

Of Wallis there was no sign.

For a moment the two men stared at her, surprised by the vision of loveliness which had burst in upon their male domain.

'Ah, there you are, my dear,' Squire Trent, struggling to his feet, held out his hand towards her. 'Now *this,* Trotter, is my new daughter-in-law.'

The thin man smirked, but the smile never reached his eyes. Squire Trent, swaying slightly, crossed the short space between them and put his arm clumsily about her waist and drew her into the room. He kicked the door shut. 'This is Mr Trotter, the horse-dealer I was telling you about.'

'I'm honoured to meet you, ma'am.' Mr Trotter rose and bowed. He was very tall, but so thin that he seemed like a reed wavering in the wind. He was a man of middle age, untidily dressed.

'Shall we go and look at the horses?' the Squire suggested.

'Shouldn't we wait for Wallis?' Adelina said.

'No—no. Come along. Trotter says he has the very horse for you, a lovely stallion...'

At that moment the door opened and Wallis strode in. He stopped short, surprised to find Adelina there. His glance took in his father's arm about her waist and the expression in his eyes hardened and his mouth tightened.

'Ar—hum,' Guy Trent grunted and let his arm fall away. He sat down heavily in his chair, picked up his tumbler of whisky and drained it, his enthusiasm gone with the arrival of his son!

Wallis said brusquely, 'Come along, then, Trotter, I haven't got all day.'

'Very good, Mr Trent.' Obediently, Trotter grabbed his hat and followed the long, angry strides of Wallis Trent. Thoughtfully, Adelina followed, leaving Squire Guy alone with his whisky bottle.

A young boy was standing holding the reins of the two horses Trotter had brought for Wallis's inspection. Adelina ran a speculative eye over them both.

'Now this would suit the lady fine,' Trotter said, patting a small brown mare on the neck. 'She's gentle and docile but strong, ma'am. She'd cause a fine lady like yourself not a bit of trouble.'

Adelina raised her left eyebrow but said nothing. Now that she had gained confidence on horseback she wanted an animal with a little more spirit than Stardust, who was getting old now. Her glance ran over the other horse. It was a white stallion and, except for its colour, the animal could have been the twin of Wallis's horse, Jupiter. Adelina's green eyes were afire with excitement. She moved towards the horse's head and stroked his nose. The proud beast tossed his head and pawed the ground. Wallis was examining the animal in great detail.

'Isn't he a fine animal, Mr Trent, sir? Now he'd be a valuable addition to your stables, wouldn't he now?'

'He would indeed, but I don't think I have need of another hunter. I'm really looking for work-horses. Have you no shires?'

'Not today, sir, but...'

'Then I'll bid you goodday.' Wallis was turning away as Adelina spoke.

'Wallis, would you object to me buying the white stallion?'

He turned abruptly. 'You, my dear? I think you'd find him too robust for you to handle. Besides, I cannot spend large sums of money on a horse we do not really need.'

'I—I could buy him myself.'

Wallis's face darkened, his jaw clenched. 'Really?' Sarcasm lined his tone. Adelina knew he must realise that any money she possessed of her own must have come from

Lynwood or from her grandfather and, either way, the knowledge angered him. But she was determined not to be intimidated. She felt the time was now when—even in this strange marriage—she must assert some individuality. She would not become a downtrodden, pathetic creature. He had married her and had given her daughter his name—and for that she was grateful—but she would not allow him to possess her mind, for her heart he could never hold.

'I am thinking of your safety, Adelina. I wouldn't be happy knowing you were riding this animal. He's too strong for any woman, however competent a horsewoman she may be.'

'I am sure I could handle him, Wallis.'

Wallis shrugged. 'Very well, then,' he said. 'But mind,' he wagged his finger at Trotter, 'the price is fair. I don't want to see my wife cheated.'

Mr Trotter's expression was pained. 'As if I would take advantage of a lady, sir!'

'You would, Trotter, you would,' Wallis remarked and began to walk towards the house. Trotter called after him, 'But what about the mare, sir? Aren't you interested in the mare?'

Wallis paused and half turned to call over

his shoulder, 'Hardly, Trotter, hardly,' and turned away again and moved on.

Trotter shrugged philosophically. 'Ah well, one sale is better than none at all.'

'What is the price?' Adelina asked.

'One hundred guineas, ma'am.'

'That's too much,' Adelina retorted sharply. 'I'll give you eighty.'

Trotter spread his hands, palms upwards. 'I'd lose on a price like that, madam. My lowest would be ninety-five.'

'Oh, come now,' Adelina purred, flashing him her most winning smile. 'I'm sure you make a handsome profit. Eighty-five.'

Trotter shook his head slowly.

Adelina sighed in mock regret and turned away. 'Well, I'm sorry, I don't believe the horse is worth that much.' She began to walk away, though her heart was pounding in case Trotter was tougher than she had imagined and would not yield.

But she had not misjudged his kind. 'Hey, wait a minute. All right—ninety—and that's my very last offer.'

Adelina whirled round. 'It's a deal!' she cried.

'Where do you want the horse taking?'

'To the stables. You know where they are.'

'Yes, ma'am.'

Mrs Wallis Trent on her white stallion soon became a familiar figure in the countryside surrounding Abbeyford. The stallion—which she named Zeus—was wild and unmanageable with anyone else, but with Adelina the animal behaved perfectly. He was her horse and hers alone. She joined the Hunt whenever it rode to hounds, and almost daily she went riding, sometimes alone, sometimes with Squire Trent and occasionally—very occasionally—with her husband.

There were two places Adelina never ventured—the abbey ruins and Lynwood Hall. Though in her heart she longed to see Lynwood again, she knew there was no turning back. He did not want her—he had made that clear. Now she was Wallis's wife and Lynwood thought all his jealous beliefs had been true.

Her greatest joy was to take her daughter and her stepson to visit Lord Royston. Here, in the disused nursery, she found a happiness and contentment she had only known in her early childhood—dim and distant memories brought to life again by two small children. And for Lord Royston, too, his days were filled with love and companionship once more.

Adelina visited the Vicarage often and, ironically, there grew between her and Sarah Smithson an uneasy friendship. It seemed as if Adelina was a tangible link between the two people who had loved each other so many years ago, who had been forced to live out their lives so close to each other and yet worlds apart.

One morning, when Adelina found herself alone with Sarah in the kitchen at the Vicarage, she said, 'Squire Trent was asking after you yesterday, Sarah.'

Sarah dropped the cup she was holding, the crash of shattering china resounding in the silent kitchen. For the first time since she had known her Adelina could see a spark in the woman's weary eyes.

'Guy? He—asked after—me?' she whispered, the words almost like a prayer of thankfulness.

Adelina felt a lump in her throat and could not stop her thoughts straying to her own lost love—Lynwood. 'Yes—yes, he wanted to know how you were and if you like being here, at the Vicarage.'

Sarah sat down at the bare, scrubbed table and folded her hands together, her eyes gazing ahead, as if instead of the kitchen about her she was seeing pictures from the past. A rare, faint smile curved her mouth. Adelina watched her, then she sat down opposite her at the table.

'Maybe I was wrong—all those years ago,' Sarah began, almost more to herself than to Adelina. 'Maybe he did love me enough. I thought, you see, that I was just another village girl to him. And then—when—I found I was with child my family were so angry—so angry. They wouldna let me even see Guy again. We weren't allowed to sort things out for oursel's. I was weak, I know, and I disappointed him. Oh, I believe he'd have stood up to his parents if I'd been strong too. But I thought—that, in years to come, he'd blame me. I thought it better that we married our own kind. And then,' her eyes clouded and her fingers twisted nervously. 'Then someone attacked Guy—in the wood—left him for dead.'

Adelina gasped but said nothing and waited for Sarah to continue. 'Sir Matthew—Guy's father—arrested my pa and sent him to gaol. He died there of gaol fever,' she finished flatly.

'However could he do that?'

'He was magistrate for this district,' she said, and the way in which she said it told Adelina that the ordinary peasant folk had been powerless under his tyranny.

'By the time—Guy recovered, I was married to Henry Smithson,' Sarah was saying. 'He's carried his bitterness agen Guy all these years and reared Evan to hate his own father.' Sarah shook her head sadly and her shoulders sagged even more as if she carried the whole burden of guilt. 'He'll not rest til he's brought trouble to the Trents.'

'Did Guy Trent manage the estate before Wallis?' Adelina asked gently.

'Not really. His father, Sir Matthew, lived to be quite an old man and was active up to the last. Wallis was almost a young man when his grandfather died and he seemed to take over straight away. Guy never really held the reins at all. Perhaps it would have been better if he had.'

'How do you mean?'

Sarah looked directly at Adelina. 'Maybe I shouldna be saying such things to you, ma'am, but you've been kind to me, and I'm grateful and—and I think you like Guy.'

Adelina nodded. 'I'm very fond of him—yes.'

'And your husband, ma'am?' Sarah asked quietly.

'I can't understand him, Sarah.' Adelina raised her shoulders slightly. 'He seems so...' She paused searching for the right word, but Sarah supplied it. 'Cold, hard, ruthless?'

Adelina sighed. 'I'm afraid so.'

Sarah nodded. 'The resentment against him in the village is growing, ma'am, and I canna do anything to prevent it.'

'Why do they dislike him so?'

'He's a hard man. The wages he pays us are poor. He never repairs the cottages he owns. An' then there's this Corn Law. Oh, I don't understand it all—it all has to do wi' politics. All I know is, the workers are worse off for't.'

'May I come and see the cottages for myself?' Adelina asked.

There was fear immediately in Sarah's eyes. 'I don't know about that, ma'am. If Henry knew I was even talkin' to you like this, he'd—he'd half kill me!'

'Some time when he's not there, then?'

'Well...' Sarah was reluctant, but a week later Adelina visited Sarah's tiny cottage.

As she entered she felt immediately closed in by the smallness, the darkness and the overpowering dankness. The hard beaten-earth floor, covered with rush mats, was cold and damp, the walls were rough and cracked. Two window panes were broken.

'What's that rustling in the roof?' Adelina asked.

'Rats!'

Adelina's mouth compressed. It was not that she had never seen such conditions before—indeed, on occasions when her father's debts had plunged them into abject poverty, she had had to suffer such hardship herself. But that she should find it here, in a village where the workmen should have been cared for by their employer, shocked and angered her.

'Sarah,' Adelina faced her, 'I don't blame the villagers for how they feel, in fact—I can't promise anything, but...'

At that moment the low door creaked open and Henry Smithson stood there. Adelina heard Sarah's gasp and could feel the woman's fear.

'Good afternoon, Mr Smithson,' Adelina said swiftly. 'I...'

'What are you doin' here?'

'I came to bring your wife her wages.' Adelina opened her reticule, thankful that she had had the foresight to have an excuse ready. She placed the coins on the rough table. She smiled at the glowering man. 'I am sorry to intrude upon you, but I missed Mrs Smithson at the Vicarage earlier.'

'Oh. I see.' He looked as if he did not believe her, but there was nothing he could do.

Adelina turned to Sarah. 'Thank you, Mrs Smithson, for all you're doing for my relatives. I do appreciate it and I'll see you are rewarded.'

As she left the cottage she heard Henry Smithson's voice rise. 'Rewarded, is it? Pah! We know what their promises are, don't we? Looked after you, didn't they? Left me to bring up their bastard...'

Adelina walked away, sorry to have brought his wrath upon Sarah's head, but she guessed that the poor woman was used to it anyway.

As Adelina left the village and walked up the lane towards the Manor, she heard hoofbeats behind her, and turned to see Wallis approaching. He reined in close beside her, causing her to step back to avoid Jupiter's restive hooves.

'Where the devil have you been?' Wallis shouted, glaring down at her.

'To the village,' Adelina replied, calmly determined not to be intimidated by him.

'You have no business there. I saw you coming out of one of the cottages. What were you doing?'

'I've been to pay Sarah Smithson her wages, that's all,' she lied glibly, using the same excuse she'd given Sarah's husband.

Wallis leaned down towards her. 'You'll keep away from the village folk. Do you hear me?'

Adelina gasped at his arrogance. Defiantly, she remained silent.

'Do you hear me, Adelina?' he shouted.

'I hear you, Wallis,' Adelina replied quietly. 'But by what right do you order me as to whom I may visit?'

'As your *husband!*'

They glared at each other, for the first time since their strange marriage had begun, openly hostile.

'I don't think much of the way you treat your employees. They are living in squalor.'

'Keep out of my affairs,' Wallis warned her.

'It is my affair. They're my grandfather's lands.'

'At the moment, maybe. But not for ever, my dear, not for ever. One way or another, they will be mine one day!'

He kicked his heels and Jupiter leapt forward, the horse's hooves narrowly missing Adelina.

She gazed after Wallis as he galloped away.

'How could I have been so foolish—even for Francesca's sake?' she murmured to herself and a picture of herself in twenty or thirty years' time—remarkably like Sarah Smithson—flashed before her mind's eye.

Adelina shuddered, pulled her cloak around her and hurried home to see the children.

CHAPTER 10

It was just over two months after their marriage that the villagers' open hostility towards Wallis Trent became more ominous.

A wild dog, or, as Wallis thought, probably two, got in among the in-lamb ewes, causing havoc. The dog, or dogs, ravaged and killed several sheep and chased others or frightened them so that quite a few aborted stillborn lambs. The slaughter was terrible to see. Adelina rode out on Zeus to the fields beyond the abbey ruins where the incident had occurred. There were six ewes dead, their bodies mutilated, their thick wool drenched with their own blood. Tiny lambs, which had never had time to draw breath, lay upon the ground, mere bundles of bones. Several other ewes were obviously very sick and did not look as though they would survive.

Adelina, unseen by him, watched Wallis sitting astride Jupiter, motionless as a stone statue, looking upon the carnage with a grim face. Beneath his arm he carried a shotgun.

Adelina urged Zeus closer until she stood beside him. 'What has caused this, Wallis? Foxes?'

'I suppose it could be—but I rather think it's a wild dog or—more likely—two. They roam and hunt in pairs.'

'Have you seen the dogs?'

'No, but I intend to find them. Now

you're here perhaps you'd better come too. Just to see what lengths your village friends will go to!'

He turned his horse away from the awful scene and Adelina followed him. She wanted to learn the truth as much as he did, though for a different reason. At walking pace, they rode side by side so that they might talk.

'The men look even more sullen than usual, Wallis. Are they upset by what has happened?'

'I doubt it,' he said shortly. 'Not one of them seems shocked by what has occurred. It was as if they'd known it was going to happen.'

Adelina gasped. 'You don't mean—you can't mean they've planned it? That they've done it on purpose?'

Wallis nodded, his expression hard. 'They'll rue the day they tried to tangle with me,' he muttered, harshly, more to himself than to her. His eyes, as he watched his workmen clearing away the carcasses, were bright with malice. That anyone—particularly anyone he considered his inferior—should dare to raise his hand against his master was beyond Wallis Trent's arrogant understanding.

His words brought a chill to her heart. Adelina said nothing but rode in thoughtful silence.

At a steady canter they rode northwards away from Abbeyford. Behind them lay the Royston farmlands, in front, rolling countryside with scarcely a farm or a cottage in sight.

'Do you farm all these fields, Wallis?'

He pointed with his riding crop. 'These directly north and east are your grandfather's lands. Over the hill to the west are Lynwood's.'

They rode on, still going northwards. The ground was frozen hard, but there had been no snow as yet. The day was bright, but bitterly cold and though Adelina was warmly dressed, she still shivered.

'Wallis, I'm cold. Let's gallop to warm ourselves.' She spurred Zeus and he leapt forward, his restless energy responding eagerly. Jupiter, not to be outdone, thundered alongside. The sharp air stung her face, but Adelina found the ride exhilarating. Across the meadows they galloped, jumping low stone walls, steadying to a canter to thread their way through a copse, rustling through the dead leaves of autumn, then out into the open fields again, with flying hooves.

At last Adelina pulled her white stallion to a steady trot. Her cheeks were rosy, her eyes bright, but Wallis did not notice.

Still frowning, he said, 'There's no sign of any dogs here. We'd better turn back now.'

They rode back towards Abbeyford in silence. As they crested the hill overlooking the village, they reined in and stood surveying the valley below them. The dead sheep had been removed, but there were still visible signs of the slaughter. Tufts of bloodstained wool and pieces of flesh littered the field.

Adelina said, 'Where would wild dogs go in the daytime? Where would they hide out?' She watched Wallis as his eyes roamed over the valley, the fields and the hillsides. She saw his gaze come to rest upon the abbey ruins. Without another word needing to be spoken between them, they both turned their horses towards the abbey.

It was wild and lonely near the crumbling, desolate ruins. The wind whipped through the broken-down building, howling mournfully. It was eerie and forbidding. Adelina shuddered.

'Stay here, Adelina. I'll take a look.' Wallis dismounted and stood a moment to load his shotgun. He did not go inside the ruins but climbed up on to a low wall. Then she noticed that he was beckoning her to join him. Swallowing the fear which rose in her throat at being so close once more to the ruins which evoked such horrific memories, Adelina dismounted and moved towards him. Without speaking, he gave her his hand to help her climb the low wall to stand beside him. Clinging to his arm she stood on the precarious, crumbling stonework and looked into the ruins. Wallis pointed and in the farthest, darkest corner she saw something move. She narrowed her eyes and gasped as, all at once, she realised there were two mangy, wild-eyed dogs in the corner—though to Adelina they looked more like wolves.

'They are *tethered!*' Wallis said in a low voice. 'Can you see the rope tying them to that ring in the wall?'

'Tethered!' Adelina repeated in a shocked whisper. Then, as she realised the full implication, horror-struck, she added, 'You mean—someone had them and—and—let them loose on your sheep?'

Wallis nodded grimly. 'It looks very

much like it. It's what I expected. Stand down now, Adelina.'

'What are you going to do?'

'Shoot them,' he replied bluntly.

Adelina climbed down from the wall and stood watching him as he raised the shotgun to his shoulder. There was a loud report which echoed through the ruins and one of the dogs fell dead. The other immediately began barking frenziedly, straining at its leash in wild terror. Seconds later, Wallis steadied his gun again. A second shot rang out and the dog ceased its barking, swayed and fell.

Slowly Wallis lowered his gun. Then he stood looking at the dogs for a moment. He turned and jumped down from the wall. Together they walked into the ruins. They stood over the dogs. They were indeed the ones which had savaged the sheep, for their rough coats were matted with blood and scraps of sheep's wool clung to their jaws. There were also a few tell-tale bones scattered nearby as if they had carried off a lamb or two to their hiding-place.

Adelina turned away, sick at heart, and went back to their horses. She watched Wallis anxiously as he walked towards her. His face was twisted with fury. His shoulders were rigid and his hands clenched. 'The dogs were obviously unleashed amongst my sheep on purpose.' He spat out the words. 'It was planned—all planned!'

'Unless someone has caught them since and tied them up here for safety,' Adelina suggested, clinging desperately to the hope that it had not been a deliberate act of vengeance.

He shook his head. 'No, it was deliberate.'

Adelina was forced to agree that he was right.

The slaughter of the sheep was the beginning of a campaign of hatred against Wallis Trent. His enemies were unseen and unknown. Whoever they were they came stealthily in the dead of night. There was a tense atmosphere of distrust throughout the village. Each villager suspected his neighbour, whilst Wallis believed that the whole village was involved in this war against him as an employer, but, above all, as a member of the hated Trent family, for no hand was laid against Abbeyford Grange and Lord Royston. The trouble was confined to Abbeyford; there was no sign of unrest at Amberly or at any of the other adjoining estates.

The vendetta went on for weeks and then months, right through the summer, and the tension mounted. Abbeyford was a village of unhappy, frightened people. Adelina mentally listed the damage caused and felt helpless to do anything. Fences were smashed and hedges torn up so that cattle escaped and wandered away. Wheels would come off farm-wagons without reason, causing a deal of damage to Wallis's vehicles. Jupiter went suddenly lame. And poaching reached frightening proportions.

One afternoon in early September, Adelina was riding Zeus through the wood behind the Manor when she heard a horse's thudding hooves behind her. Startled, she turned to see Squire Trent galloping towards her through the trees. He pulled hard on the reins and his horse halted abruptly beside her. It tossed its head and stamped angrily at its rider's rough treatment of it. Zeus, too, became restive.

'Whoa there, boy,' Guy shouted and grinned broadly at Adelina.

Adelina smiled warmly at him. 'Shall we ride a little way together?' she offered.

'I'd be honoured, my dear. If you'll permit me, I'll show you something worth your while. You like a bit of sport, eh?' His eyes were feverishly bright. Adelina hesitated.

'Come on,' he said and spurred his horse forward. Adelina followed, a little reluctantly.

As they reached the edge of the wood, Guy Trent said, 'We'd best leave the horses here, Adelina.'

'Why?'

'It's all right. You're safe with me. But we must go quietly, we don't want to be seen.'

'I don't understand you. Where are you taking me?'

'To the abbey ruins.'

'No!' Adelina cried out. 'I won't come.'

'It's all right, my dear,' he said again. 'I just want you to see a sport the village menfolk enjoy.' He pointed. 'Look, several are making their way there now. Only we mustn't be seen. We must stay here in the trees until all the men are inside and then we'll creep up and watch from a place I know where they can't see us. Don't worry—I often come, but I always take care they don't know I'm there.'

'But what is it?'

'You'll see. I want it to be a surprise.'

They waited some time, watching from the shelter of the trees as men from the village arrived in twos and threes and slipped into the abbey ruins.

'There—I can't see anyone else coming. Come on. Follow me and don't make a noise whatever you do.'

Adelina, still wary, followed Squire Trent. He skirted the ruins and went round to the opposite side from that overlooking the valley. They climbed a small bank at the top of which were some bushes growing against a wall which was not so badly broken down as some of the others. Guy pushed his way through, holding the branches aside for Adelina. They came up against the wall.

'Here, over here,' he whispered, and Adelina saw him crouching down to peer through a peephole in the wall. Curiosity overcame her doubts and she crouched down beside him. Below them in the abbey, in what had once been one of the larger rooms, about twenty-five to thirty men were gathered. The rubble had been cleared away from the ground and they were all standing in a circle with a clear space in the centre.

At first Adelina could not think what it was they were going to do. Then on either side of the ring she saw two men each holding a fine cockerel. On the cocks' feet were fitted metal spurs. The birds were struggling to free themselves, but the men held them fast, whilst a third man went round the others taking money from them.

Adelina put her mouth close to the squire's ear and whispered, 'What are they doing?'

In turn he whispered to her. 'Cock-fighting. The man in the middle taking money is taking bets on which will be the victor. I fancy the one on the left. Look at those legs! He'll tear the other one to pieces.'

Adelina was not quite sure what he meant or exactly what was going to happen until she saw the fight begin. The man in the centre of the ring completed his bet-collecting and then the two cockerels were released. In a wild flurry of beating wings, necks outstretched, the cocks flew at each other. Their sharp, pointed beaks pecked viciously at each other's head and neck. Then, one backed off a little and then surged forward. His wings flapping and both feet clear of the ground, he aimed the metal spurs straight at his opponent's chest. The wounded cock staggered. Adelina clapped her hand to her mouth to still a horrified scream which threatened to escape her lips. It was not that she was squeamish, but the bloodthirsty attack was so unexpected.

'Come on, come on,' Guy urged in a whisper, for the wounded cock was the one which he had thought would win. Adelina glanced at him. His eyes were bright with excitement. He ran his tongue over his dry lips.

The noise from the watching men below was deafening. They were shouting or cursing whichever cock they had backed. Again the first cock made another lunge towards the already bleeding one, but he dodged away at the last moment, so that the assailant fell on to the ground instead, momentarily losing his balance. Taking swift advantage, the other cock flew at him from behind and mounted his back, digging in his spurs. The shouts increased as the fight swung this way and that, with first one bird seeming the strongest, then the other. All the time the watchers—all except the two hidden in the bushes—shouted encouragement.

At last the fight was over when one of the cocks lay, a bleeding mass of feathers, upon the ground. The other could hardly be said to strut proudly, for it staggered around hardly able to stand either.

Squire Trent nodded with satisfaction. 'There, I told you that one would win. Wish I'd had a sovereign on it. Good fight, wasn't it?'

Adelina shuddered. 'I suppose so, if you like that sort of thing.'

He looked at her in surprise. 'I thought you liked a bit of sport. You joined the Hunt.'

She grimaced. 'I joined the Hunt for the riding and the social gathering. I can't say I relish the kill very much.'

'Oh, well, I'm sorry I brought you then,' he said huffily.

'I'm glad to have seen it,' Adelina tried to placate him. 'Thank you for bringing me. I heard tell George Washington used to enjoy the sport.'

'Really?' the squire said, somewhat mollified.

'What do we do now?'

'Wait until they've all gone before we

leave or we'll risk being seen.'

But the village men showed no sign of dispersing. In fact, the atmosphere became quieter, more serious, as if, the sport over for the day, they now had business to discuss. They talked amongst themselves for some five minutes whilst Squire Trent grumbled. 'Whatever are they playing at? Why don't they get off home? They don't usually dally once the fight's done. Can't understand it...'

At that moment his whispered mutterings were cut short by the arrival through the broken, stone archway of another man. Squire Trent's mouth dropped open and his eyes bulged in surprise. Adelina, tired of watching through the peephole, was now sitting with her back against the wall just waiting until her companion should give the word that all was clear for them to leave. She saw the strange expression upon his face and sat upright again.

'What is it?' she hissed.

He put his forefinger to his lips and Adelina was surprised to see that his hand trembled. Mystified and intrigued she twisted round to see the cause. She almost cried out as she recognised the man who had just come into the ruins and now stood on a low wall some three feet high so that he could address the other men and be clearly seen and heard by them.

'Evan,' Adelina whispered hoarsely. 'It's Evan Smithson!'

Squire Trent nodded soberly. 'I wonder where the devil he's sprung from again?'

A shadowy incident, just out of reach of her conscious mind, seemed to flicker across Adelina's memory, as if she ought to know and yet she could just not remember...

Evan was speaking now. Squire Trent and Adelina bent forward, their faces close together, to listen. There was something ominous about this meeting of the village men, and both were anxious to learn what it was.

'My friends,' Evan was shouting, spreading his arms wide in a gesture of grand eloquence. 'I have come here today to show you that I am alive. I left Abbeyford—vowing never to return. But, my friends, I kept thinking of you all under the whip of that tyrant, Wallis Trent. So I came back.' He grinned. 'I have been back several months!' And Adelina knew instinctively that Evan Smithson had been behind the mysterious happenings against the Trents. 'You all know I have reason enough to hate him and his kind,' he was saying. 'And so have you, if you think on't.'

He prodded his forefinger towards the men. A low murmuring ran amongst them. 'He doesn't care if you work yourselves into an early grave, or if you've a roof over your head or enough food in your bellies, or whether your children run barefoot and shiver in winter and die of starvation.'

The murmurings grew louder.

'Does he put more money in your pockets, my friends? He's lining his own whilst you starve. Does *his* family live on a diet of rye bread, potatoes and skim-milk? No, his son will eat meat every day, if he wants. When did your children last eat *meat?*'

'We share a pig now and again,' someone muttered, but Evan, if he heard, ignored the remark.

'And so, my fellow peasants, I say it is time for revolution. It is time we stood up for our rights as human beings instead of being slaves to the gentry. The whole country wants Parliamentary reform. We want the Corn Law abolished.'

The cries of assent rang through the

crumbling walls, and Adelina and Guy Trent exchanged a look of deep anxiety. Only one voice tried to bring a note of sanity. 'Aye, but Trents is cattle-farmers. This 'ere Corn Law won't mek no difference to us.' But he was quickly silenced.

Evan's tirade was relentless. 'Last week I went to a meeting near Manchester—at Peterloo—only about twenty miles from here. A peaceful meeting it was, of farm labourers from hereabouts and men from the cotton mills too. It wasn't intended to be a riot or a rebellion. Men took their families, their wives and little children—even babes in arms. But what did the magistrates do? They called out the yeomanry, who charged amongst the people killin' and maiming. I tell you, my friends, if you could 'ave seen the sight afterwards—the field was littered like a battlefield. Men wounded and dying, women trampled by the horses, children orphaned in the space of a few seconds, crying pitifully. It was a massacre, a bloody massacre!'

The angry resentment and hatred was now written upon every face. The murmurings grew to a cry for revenge.

Evan held up his hand and the noise abated. In a lower, more conspiratorial voice, he said, 'But *our* grievances are closer to home than with Parliament, aren't they, my friends? We will meet on the village green on Saturday next and go to the Manor to ask for, no, to demand a better wage and better conditions. The Trents sit up there in their grand Manor living off the fruits of your labours whilst you live out your dismal lives with scarcely enough to eat in your tumble-down cottages—which he owns.'

'What if he wun't do aught?'

'Then we'll have to get a little nasty, won't us?' Evan's face twisted into such an expression of bitter hatred that Adelina shuddered, remembering all too clearly how, once, she had seen that same expression on Evan's face—at very close proximity!

'What d'you mean?'

Evan shrugged. 'We'll burn his stacks, his barn, even his fine house, an' see how *he* likes being poor!'

'No, no, it's too much.'

'No—we munna do harm.'

'He deserves it—he dunna care for us.'

'Evan's right. After all—he should know.'

The remarks flew furiously amongst the men, only a few rising clearly to Adelina's ears above the general babble.

Evan caught and held on to the last remark.

'Yes, I should know. For am I not a Trent by birth? But you all know what that drunken old sot did? Left an innocent village girl to live a life of shame just because he had to marry one of his own class. An' the older ones among you will remember me grandpa—how he was sent to gaol for summat he didna do, an' how he died there!'

Adelina saw Squire Trent's face turn a deathly grey colour and a soft moan escaped his lips. 'Oh, Sarah, Sarah! What have we done? Is it not enough how we have suffered all these years apart?'

Adelina was moved to take his hand and hold it comfortingly. She was hearing proof from his own lips that Squire Trent had really loved Sarah. What pain Evan's actions must be causing him, for, after all, he was his son!

At last the meeting broke up and the men sneaked away out of the ruins back towards Abbeyford. Evan Smithson disappeared in the opposite direction. Not until everyone had been gone for some minutes did Guy Trent and Adelina dare to move their cramped limbs and leave their hiding-place.

The hillside was deserted as they hurried across the open space to the wood.

'Whatever shall we do?' Adelina panted as she took little running steps in her haste to escape from the scene she had just witnessed. The horrors of the cock-fight were completely obliterated by the mutinous meeting which had followed.

'We—must tell Wallis.'

'Yes, yes, of course, we must tell Wallis,' she agreed, but added, 'but what will *he* do?'

'What are you going to do?' Adelina repeated her question to Wallis some time later as she and Squire Trent stood facing him across the smooth leather-top of the desk in his study. They had recounted the full story of the scene they had witnessed. Between them they were able to repeat what had been said almost word for word. She bit her lip, waiting apprehensively for his reply.

'I shall follow the good example of the Manchester magistrates and call out the yeomanry.'

'Oh, no, Wallis. You can't possibly do that—not against your own people.'

Wallis, a fearsome frown upon his face, leaned towards her threateningly. 'My people? You dare to call them *my people* after what they have done to me these last months. It started with the sheep and, every week since something has been destroyed or stolen, or animals injured. *My people!* Pah!' He thumped one fist against the palm of his other hand. 'Adelina, you will not interfere. You hear me?'

Adelina stared at him in disbelief. Was she really married to this cold, heartless man who would call out the soldiers against his own workers?

She turned away sick at heart.

For two days Adelina worried and fretted over what she could do to prevent the tragedy which was sure to occur.

There was a stillness in the air, an oppressiveness, as if everyone and everything were waiting—waiting for the storm of hatred and revenge and arrogance to unleash itself. She feared for the safety of the children. Jamie Trent and her own daughter. If the rioters meant what they said—then the whole Trent family was in danger.

On the Friday, Adelina could bear the suspense no longer. When she knew Wallis was out, she gave orders for the carriage to be made ready and brought to the side entrance. Hastily she thrust some garments for the children and herself into a portmanteau and instructed Jane to do likewise. 'You'll be staying at Abbeyford Grange for a few nights. I'm sure Lord Royston won't mind.'

'Aren't you coming, ma'am?'

'I'm taking you there, but—I don't know yet.'

Once the children were safe, Adelina told herself, perhaps she would be able to think more rationally.

She did not tell anyone else in the household what she was doing—Wallis would be angry enough when he found out.

As the carriage passed through the village, the strangely silent street made Adelina's nerves tremble with dread. When they arrived at Abbeyford Grange, Adelina sent Jane with the children to find the housekeeper while she went in search of Lord Royston.

She flew through the hallway and into the drawing-room.

'Grandfather,' she cried, 'Grandfather...' Then she stopped in surprise as she saw that her grandfather had a visitor.

The world seemed to rock beneath her feet as she breathed his name. 'Francis! Oh, Francis!'

CHAPTER 11

The Earl of Lynwood had turned at the sound of her voice. For a moment, across the room, their eyes met and held. She read the longing in his gaze and for a moment all the love in her heart was in her eyes for him to see. There was a flash of exultation, of love, in his. She stood before him, a woman, beautiful, yet with the maturity and serenity and kindliness that Life's harsh experience had taught her. In her lovely face was the strength of a fine character.

How could he have ever thought she was like Caroline, who, though equally lovely, had been selfish and ruthless?

The pain of his final loss of Adelina on her marriage to Wallis Trent and the realisation that it had been his own blind stupidity which had forced her to take such a disastrous step, had finally—once and for all—obliterated his boyish memories.

Ironically, when at last Lynwood realised that it was Adelina he loved for herself alone, it was too late for she was the wife of Wallis Trent!

Lord Royston broke the spell. 'Whatever is the matter, my child?'

'Oh—I—yes. Grandfather—it's Wallis. He's going to—to call out the yeomanry. The villagers—they're planning to march to the Manor and he—he intends to quell what he thinks will be a riot with the use of soldiers.'

Lord Royston and Lynwood exchanged anxious glances.

'This is serious, my lord,' Lynwood said earnestly.

Lord Royston nodded, his old eyes full of concern. He thumped his stick on the floor. 'The stupid, arrogant fool! What does he think he's playing at? And how's he managed to call them out? He's not a magistrate, is he?'

'No,' Lynwood answered soberly. 'But you are!'

'Well, I haven't given any such order.'

'No, I realise that. But Trent wields power and influence, often in your name.'

'Does he indeed? The scoundrel!'

Lynwood glanced at Adelina as if to see what effect her grandfather's words had upon her. She moved forward and said softly, 'Grandfather, it's the villagers I'm afraid for. They're angry and bitter and resentful, roused by Evan Smithson.'

'Who?'

'Evan Smithson. Guy Trent's—illegitimate son.'

Adelina glanced at Lynwood. They were both remembering Evan, the abbey ruins and Lynwood's fight with him—and the reason for it.

'Good lord! So he's at the bottom of this, is he?' Lord Royston murmured, knowing nothing of their memories.

Swiftly, Adelina told them of the scene Squire Trent and she had witnessed at the abbey ruins. 'We told Wallis, thinking he'd be able to handle the situation, but instead all he would say is that they deserve all they get and he'll put an end to it once and for all.'

She sat down heavily and dropped her head into her hands. 'There will be such bloodshed and suffering. I don't know how he can be so—so cruel. I can't bear it!'

She felt Lynwood's hand upon her shoulder. 'I'll see what I can do. But it's late now, I doubt I'll be in time.'

Adelina lifted her tear-streaked face and covered his hand with her own. 'Oh, Francis, thank you.'

Swiftly he bent and kissed her, their lips clinging desperately, hungrily, for a moment and then he turned and hurried from the room.

Adelina and her grandfather looked at each other sadly. 'Oh, Grandfather—what have I done?' she said heavily, not expecting him to answer. Then briskly she roused herself. She could not let herself wallow in the self-pity the sight of Francis had aroused in her. There was no time now for indulging in thoughts of what might have been.

'I hope you don't mind—I've brought the children here to stay for a few days.'

'Of course not, my dear. And you must stay here too.'

'No,' Adelina said quietly. 'I must go back. There may be something I can do, even now, to prevent it.'

'I wish you wouldn't go,' Lord Royston said, then he sighed. 'But in some ways you're too much like your mother to take notice of me—but not in every way, my dear, dear girl.'

Adelina bent and kissed his bald head. 'Dear Grandfather,' she murmured and then hurried away.

She mounted Zeus, which she had brought for her return, and left Abbeyford Grange.

As she entered the hall at the Manor, Wallis was waiting for her. He grasped her arm in a vice-like grip, and half dragged her into his study. Slamming the door behind him, he turned upon her. 'Where is my son? What have you done with him?'

Courageously, Adelina squared her shoulders and faced him. 'I have taken both children, and Jane, to Abbeyford Grange. They will be safe there.'

'Then you will fetch them back at once,' he said, his teeth clenched, his eyes bright with anger.

'Not until the danger is over.'

Menacingly, he said. 'Do you think, madam, that I cannot protect my own son? You will fetch him back—*now!*'

'I—will—not,' Adelina said meeting his almost maniacal wrath with an outward show of fearlessness.

Wallis raised his right arm and with the back of his hand dealt her a stinging blow across the face. She fell against a chair, knocking it over as she tumbled to the floor. He stood over her, powerful, arrogant and utterly ruthless. Roughly, he grasped her arm and pulled her to her feet, almost dislocating her shoulder. Adelina cried out in pain.

At that moment the door opened and his father came in. He stopped in amazement. 'What the devil...? Wallis, have you taken leave of your senses?'

'Get out,' Wallis snarled. But as he turned momentarily towards his father he relaxed his grip upon Adelina. All her instincts for survival, which had saved her so often in the waterfront taverns, rose to the surface. Twisting away, she pushed past Squire Trent and ran through the hall. She heard Wallis shout, was dimly aware of a scuffle as the older man attempted to stop Wallis following her. Out of the front door and down the steps. Zeus was being led away by a stable-boy.

'Wait, wait!' Adelina cried, desperately afraid her shaking legs would not carry her. Wallis was at the door as she reached her horse. The boy took one look at his angry master, bent quickly and cupped his hands.

'Here, missus, quick!'

Gratefully, Adelina put her foot into his hands and hoisted herself on to the horse. She grasped the reins and as Wallis ran towards them, she kicked at Zeus. As she galloped away out of reach she turned back to see Wallis attacking the stable-lad, venting his frustration on the innocent boy.

Adelina galloped down the lane, through the village and up to Abbeyford Grange.

It was only when she knew she was safe, that the fear and terror overwhelmed her. 'I can never go back to him,' she whispered to herself. 'Never!'

Saturday dawned, and, as if to match the ominous situation, the weather was sultry. Black clouds hung over the village and yet there was no rain. Thunder rumbled in the far distance and the air was breathless.

Adelina worried the hours away, watching from the long windows in the library at the Grange. As it began to grow dusk, she could see, far below, lighted torches moving towards the village green, until there seemed to be a pool of flickering light in the centre of the village.

There had been no word from Lynwood. Adelina did not know whether he had prevented the yeomanry from being called out or not.

'I must warn them,' she whispered. 'I cannot let this foolishness go any further.'

She hurried upstairs to dress herself. With shaking fingers she put on her dark riding-habit and black cloak. Pulling the hood well down over her face, she let herself quietly out of the side door and out on to the terrace. She hurried down the steps and through the rose garden and out of the door in the wall. Slipping and stumbling, Adelina ran down the sloping field towards the village.

As she neared the green, she heard on the still air the sound of many voices and saw the gathering of men, several holding flaming torches. She watched them assemble, form into ranks and begin to march in reasonably orderly fashion out of the village, and up the lane towards Abbeyford Manor. Evan Smithson, his torch held high like a banner, led them.

She began to run after them. 'Evan, Evan! Wait! I must tell you...'

The men faltered and several stopped

at the sound of her voice to look around. She moved into the light from their torches and stood facing Evan. Close behind him she could see Henry Smithson, his face grim.

'Why, if it ain't the Lady of the Manor hersel'!' Evan said. 'And what might you be doin' out on a dangerous night like this'n? Your dear husband should take better care of you, my lovely Adelina.'

'Evan—all of you,' she cried, 'you must listen to me. Wallis has called out the yeomanry to put down your riot.'

For a moment there was silence, then Evan laughed. 'Tekin' a tip from the Peterloo magistrates, is he?' He paused a moment as if thinking rapidly. 'I don't believe you. He hasn't the power. Only your grandfather has that power. Has *he...?*'

'No—no, he wouldn't do such a thing. But we think Wallis may have—may have used Lord Royston's name to influence those concerned. Lord Lynwood has tried to stop it, but—but I—we haven't heard from him.'

'Huh, expect us to believe any of *his* sort would try to stop it?' Henry Smithson growled. 'Tek no notice of her.'

'Lord Lynwood is a good man,' Adelina said quietly.

'What about Trent—your husband? Is he "a good man"?' Evan asked.

'I...' Adelina could not speak. She was torn apart. Her shoulders slumped and weariness swept over her. 'I came to warn you. I don't want there to be bloodshed.'

Evan moved closer. In the light from his torch she saw again the face of the man who had caused her so much unhappiness. And yet she had been moved to try to save him and his friends. Whatever heartache Evan Smithson had caused her, she could not allow him to walk towards the destruction his own half-brother planned.

'I think *he's* sent you. He's only using you to save himself. I don't believe he could call out the yeomanry, though I know he would. So,' he grasped hold of her arm, giving it a vicious wrench and twisting it behind her so that she was obliged to walk in front of him. 'We'll take you with us, my lovely. Perhaps with you as hostage, he'll listen more readily to what we have to say.'

Adelina sobbed with fear and frustration, panting for breath as Evan pushed her in front of him. Every limb in her body was trembling and her heart was thudding painfully.

With Evan once more leading them but now with Adelina in the very front, the men resumed their march towards the Manor.

Without warning there came through the night the sound of thudding hooves—but the sound did not come from the Manor stables. It was the noise of many horses being ridden hard. Then Adelina saw them—dark, swiftly-moving shadows emerging from the trees at the top of the hill, swooping recklessly, down the hillside towards the band of village men carrying torches. For a moment time seemed to stand still. The village men stopped and with one accord looked up at the brigade of yeomanry charging down upon them.

'My God! He *has* done it!' Evan muttered.

The horses came nearer and nearer and the village men, the mesmerism broken, gave wild cries of terror and began to flee in all directions. Torches were thrown aside and the reason for their march upon the Manor forgotten as they fled to save their own lives. Adelina stood quite still, so filled with terror that she could not move.

She faced certain death, brought about by her own husband!

Then she felt herself grasped round the waist by Evan and thrown bodily over a stone wall. He jumped over after her and crouched down for protection. She lay where she had fallen, the breath knocked from her body. The horsemen were upon the men, chasing and harassing like huntsmen after a fox. Screams of fear and pain filled the night air as some of the men were trampled upon by the horses or caught by the flashing sabres of the yeoman. The carnage, the screaming, the horses trampling and rearing, seemed to go on for ever. Only Adelina, saved by Evan, and Evan himself, were safe behind the stone wall.

Then suddenly it was over. The cavalry re-formed and rode back the way they had come, leaving a scene of devastation.

Evan rose and stood looking at the scene. Adelina, too, pulled herself up. In the moonlight she could see the dark shapes of men lying on the ground, hear their groans and the cries of those badly injured.

'My God!' whispered Evan.

Adelina moaned aloud. 'How could he

do it? How *could* he?'

Grimly, Evan picked up one of the torches still alight, its flame licking the grass. He looked down at her, and now there was no hatred towards her. 'I'm sorry. I should have believed you. Stay here and you won't be hurt...'

'Where are you going?' Panic rose again. 'What are you going to do?'

'Never mind. Just stay here.' There was a lust for revenge on his face as he turned away.

'Evan—no—you mustn't.' She scrambled after him, but he was running now, too fast for her, towards the Manor.

'Evan—no!'

Adelina stumbled and fell against a prickly bush, which tore at her hands and face and wrenched at her clothes. Weeping and sobbing with frustration, she struggled to free herself. Then as she stumbled on, she saw the first flames leaping from the stack-yard at the side of the Manor.

'Oh, no!' she breathed. 'Evan's setting fire to the Manor. My God!'

She ran, fear giving her added strength. By the time she reached the yard, she saw Evan silhouetted against the orange glow moving towards the stables.

'No—Evan—not the horses.' Then she saw Wallis's tall figure, saw Evan turn to face him, saw them pause, stare at each other. Evan turned and threw his lighted torch upon the stable roof as Wallis leapt upon him, too late to prevent his action.

They crashed to the ground and rolled over and over. Burning wisps of straw floated everywhere and the air was filled with acrid fumes. The stable roof began to burn, unnoticed by the two grappling men.

'Wallis, Wallis, the horses,' Adelina cried desperately.

Then she heard the sound of horse's hooves and turned to see Lynwood galloping towards her. He threw himself from his horse and ran to her. 'Adelina—my darling. You're safe—thank God.'

Oblivious to the fact that her husband was close by, Lynwood folded her into his embrace, burying his face against her hair, murmuring, 'Adelina—oh, Adelina.'

For one blissful moment she clung to him, suspended in time, one moment from all eternity when they were locked together in pure, overflowing love for each other, the world forgotten save their own two selves.

Then brutal reality awoke them, as a roof timber of the stable crashed to the ground, and the horses in the burning building kicked and fought to release themselves from their stalls, the sound they made like screams of terror.

'The horses!' Adelina made to pull herself away, but Lynwood held her fast.

'No, Adelina. You cannot help them. You'd be killed.'

Wallis seemed suddenly to realise what was happening and pushing Evan Smithson from him he ran towards the burning stables.

'Trent—don't be a fool!' Lynwood shouted, but Adelina could utter no word. She could only stand and watch as the tall, broad figure of her husband rushed headlong into the flames towards the stall holding his horse, Jupiter.

Evan Smithson fled and Lynwood, seeing him go, made a lunge forward to prevent him, but it was Adelina's turn now to restrain him. 'No, Francis. Let him go.'

Lynwood looked down at her in amazement. 'Let him—go?'

Adelina nodded. 'He saved my life—back there. When the yeomanry charged the men, I was with them—in the very front. Evan saved my life.'

Lynwood held her face cupped in his hands and kissed her lips gently. 'Then—for that alone—he deserves to go free,' he murmured. 'Adelina—there's so much I want to say...' But at that moment Wallis appeared once more, trying to lead out his stallion from the burning stable. The animal was hurt and wild with terror. It reared and plunged and kicked. For a moment Wallis seemed about to master Jupiter, then, as another roof timber crashed down behind the animal and the flames roared with renewed force, the horse reared, standing on his hind legs, a colossal black shape, its hooves flailing, to come crashing down—its full weight upon Wallis.

Adelina screamed and Lynwood leapt forward as Jupiter, free now, galloped away.

Wallis lay quite still, his head at a peculiar angle, blood pouring from his head, his eyes open, staring, his mouth gaping.

Gently, Lynwood felt for his pulse, then his heart. 'I think he's dead, Adelina.'

'Dead?' she repeated stupidly.

Then, quietly and without warning, she fainted.

Adelina awoke in a strange room—a bedroom at Abbeyford Grange. She became aware of Jane sitting close by.

'Oh, madam, you're awake.'

'The children?' was Adelina's first question.

'Quite safe.'

And—and,' Adelina raised herself on one elbow. 'Lord Lynwood?'

'He's safe. He's downstairs, ma'am, pacing up and down like a caged lion, waiting for you to wake up, but—but...'

'Yes?' Panic caught at her again.

'Mr Wallis, ma'am. He—he's dead.'

The panic faded. She lay back and sighed deeply. 'I know. I remember,' she said heavily. 'Was anyone else killed?'

'Three from the village, ma'am, and several badly injured. Henry Smithson—he may not live, but, if he does, he'll never walk again. Crippled for life, he'll be.'

Adelina groaned. 'What about Evan?'

'Oh, he's gone again, ma'am, as quick as he come. Mind you, they reckon he's been living in Amberly for quite some time. Married he is, they say, with children.

Not that I know him, ma'am, but I've heard all the gossip up at the Manor.' She glanced at Adelina. 'He's been planning all this for a long time. He's used the unrest of the times for his own purpose. To bring revenge on the Trents.'

'Yes, yes,' Adelina said heavily. She frowned. 'And now I remember. I think I saw him once—in Amberly. I saw this man in the shadows and he seemed familiar. But I never thought, never dreamt, it was Evan. I hope this time he's gone for good!'

She lay back and closed her eyes and, as the heartache began to recede, the warm and comforting knowledge enveloped her.

Downstairs Lynwood was waiting.